Francesca Simon

THE AMAZING ADVENTURES OF HORRID HENRY

Illustrated by Tony Ross

Orion
Children's Books

For Marvellous Martin, without whom Horrid Henry
would have never happened

First published in Great Britain in 2008 and 2009 as
Horrid Henry's House of Horrors and *Horrid Henry's Dreadful Deeds*
by Orion Children's Books
a division of the Orion Publishing Group Ltd
Orion House
5 Upper St Martin's Lane
London WC2H 9EA
An Hachette Livre UK Company

Text © Francesca Simon 1994, 1995, 1998, 2000, 2002,
2002, 2003, 2004, 2005, 2006, 2008
Illustrations © Tony Ross 1994, 1995, 1998, 2000, 2002,
2003, 2004, 2005, 2006, 2008, 2009

The Orion Publishing Group's policy is to use papers that are natural,
renewable, and recyclable products and made from wood grown in
sustainable forests. The logging and manufacturing processes are expected
to conform to the environmental regulations of the country of origin.

ISBN 978 1 40724 467 9

Printed and bound in Thailand

www.orionbooks.co.uk

Contents

HEROIC HENRY'S BEST PICTURES

Grandma

Dog

Peter

Great-Aunt Greta

Rich Aunt Ruby

Mum

Dad

Stuck-up Steve

HORRID HENRY'S CAR JOURNEY

'Henry! We're waiting!'

'Henry! Get down here!'

'Henry! I'm warning you!'

Horrid Henry sat on his bed and scowled. His mean, horrible parents could warn him all they liked. He wasn't moving.

'Henry! We're going to be late,' yelled Mum.

'Good!' shouted Henry.

'Henry! This is your final warning,' yelled Dad.

'I don't want to go to Polly's!' screamed Henry. 'I want to go to Ralph's birthday party.'

Mum stomped upstairs.

'Well you can't,' said Mum. 'You're coming to the christening, and that's that.'

'NO!' screeched Henry. 'I hate Polly, I hate babies, and I hate you!'

Henry had been a page-boy at the wedding of his cousin, Prissy Polly, when she'd married Pimply Paul. Now they had a prissy, pimply baby, Vomiting Vera.

Henry had met Vera once before. She'd thrown up all over him. Henry had hoped never to see her again until she was grown up and behind bars, but no such luck. He had to go and watch her be dunked in a vat of water, on the same day that Ralph was having a birthday party at Goo-Shooter World. Henry had been

longing for ages to go to Goo-Shooter World. Today was his chance. His only chance. But no. Everything was ruined.

Perfect Peter poked his head round the door.

'*I'm* all ready, Mum,' said Perfect Peter. His shoes were polished, his teeth were brushed, and his hair neatly combed. 'I know how annoying it is to be kept waiting when you're in a rush.'

'Thank you, darling Peter,' said Mum. 'At least *one* of my children knows how to behave.'

Horrid Henry roared and attacked. He was a swooping vulture digging his claws into a dead mouse.

'AAAAAAAAAEEEEE!'

squealed Peter.

'Stop being horrid, Henry!' said Mum.

'No one told me it was today!' screeched Henry.

'Yes we did,' said Mum. 'But you weren't paying attention.'

'As usual,' said Dad.

'*I* knew we were going,' said Peter.

'I DON'T WANT TO GO TO POLLY'S!' screamed Henry. 'I want to go to Ralph's!'

'Get in the car – NOW!' said Dad.

'Or no TV for a year!' said Mum.

Eeek! Horrid Henry stopped wailing. No TV for a

year. Anything was better than that.

Grimly, he stomped down the stairs and out of the front door. They wanted him in the car. They'd have him in the car.

'Don't slam the door,' said Mum.

Slam!

Horrid Henry pushed Peter away from the car door and scrambled for the right-hand side behind the driver. Perfect Peter grabbed his legs and tried to climb over him.

Victory! Henry got there first.

Henry liked sitting on the right-hand side so he could watch the speedometer.

Peter liked sitting on the right-hand side so he could watch the speedometer.

'Mum,' said Peter. 'It's my turn to sit on the right.'

'No it isn't,' said Henry. 'It's mine.'

'Mine!'

'Mine!'

'We haven't even left and already you're fighting?' said Dad.

'You'll take turns,' said Mum. 'You can swap after we stop.'

Vroom.
Vroom.

Dad started the car.

The doors locked.

Horrid Henry was trapped.

But wait. Was there a glimmer of hope? Was there a teeny tiny chance? What was it Mum always said when he and Peter were squabbling in the car? 'If you don't stop fighting I'm going to turn around and go home!' And wasn't home just exactly where he wanted to be? All he had to do was to do what he did best.

'Could I have a story tape please?' said Perfect Peter.

'No! I want a music tape,' said Horrid Henry.

'I want "Mouse Goes to Town",' said Peter.

'I want "Driller Cannibals' Greatest Hits",' said Henry.

'Story!'

'Music!'

'Story!'

'Music!'

SMACK! SMACK!

'WAAAAAAA!'

'Stop it, Henry,' said Mum.

'Tell Peter to leave me alone!' screamed Henry.

'Tell Henry to leave *me* alone!' screamed Peter.

'Leave each other alone,' said Mum.

Horrid Henry glared at Perfect Peter.

Perfect Peter glared at Horrid Henry.

Horrid Henry stretched. Slowly, steadily, centimetre by centimetre, he spread out into Peter's area.

'Henry's on my side!'

'No I'm not!'

'Henry, leave Peter alone,' said Dad. 'I mean it.'

'I'm not doing anything,' said Henry. 'Are we there yet?'

'No,' said Dad.

Thirty seconds passed.

'Are we there yet?' said Horrid Henry.

'No!' said Mum.

'Are we there yet?' said Horrid Henry.

'NO!' screamed Mum and Dad.

'We only left ten minutes ago,' said Dad.

Ten minutes! Horrid Henry felt as if they'd been travelling for hours.

'Are we a quarter of the way there yet?'

'NO!'

'Are we halfway there yet?'

'NO!!'

'How much longer until we're halfway there?'

'Stop it, Henry!' screamed Mum.

'You're driving me crazy!' screamed Dad. 'Now be quiet and leave us alone.'

Henry sighed. Boy, was this boring. Why didn't they have a decent car, with built-in video games, movies, and jacuzzi? That's just what he'd have, when he was king.

Softly, he started to hum under his breath.

'Henry's humming!'

'Stop being horrid, Henry!'

'I'm not doing anything,' protested Henry. He lifted his foot.

'MUM!' squealed Peter. 'Henry's kicking me.'

'Are you kicking him, Henry?'

'Not yet,' muttered Henry. Then he screamed.

'Mum! Peter's looking out of my window!'

'Dad! Henry's looking out of *my* window.'

'Peter breathed on me.'

'Henry's breathing loud on purpose.'

'Peter's on my side!'

'Henry's staring at me.'

'Tell him to stop!' screamed Henry and Peter.

Mum's face was red.

Dad's face was red.

'That's it!' screamed Dad.

'I can't take this any more!' screamed Mum.

Yes! thought Henry. We're going to turn back!

But instead of turning round, the car screeched to a halt at the motorway services.

'We're going to take a break,' said Mum. She looked exhausted.

'Who needs a wee?' said Dad. He looked even worse.

'Me,' said Peter.

'Henry?'

'No,' said Henry. He wasn't a baby. He knew when he needed a wee and he didn't need one now.

'This is our only stop, Henry,' said Mum. 'I think you should go.'

'NO!' screamed Henry. Several people looked up. 'I'll wait in the car.'

Mum and Dad were too tired to argue. They disappeared into the services with Peter.

Rats. Despite his best efforts, it looked like Mum and Dad were going to carry on. Well, if he couldn't make them turn back, maybe he could *delay* them? Somehow? Suddenly Henry had a wonderful, spectacular idea. It couldn't be easier, and it was guaranteed to work. He'd miss the christening!

Mum, Dad, and Peter got back in the car. Mum drove off.

'I need a wee,' said Henry.

'Not now, Henry.'

'I NEED A WEE!' screamed Henry. 'NOW!'

Mum headed back to the services.

Dad and Henry went to the toilets.

'I'll wait for you outside,' said Dad. 'Hurry up or we'll be late.'

Late! What a lovely word.

Henry went into the toilet and locked the door. Then he waited. And waited. And waited.

Finally, he heard Dad's grumpy voice.

'Henry? Have you fallen in?'

Henry rattled the door.

'I'm locked in,' said Henry. 'The door's stuck. I can't get out.'

'Try, Henry,' pleaded Dad.

'I have,' said Henry. 'I guess they'll have to break the door down.'

That should take a few hours. He settled himself on the toilet seat and got out a comic.

'Or you could just crawl underneath the partition into the next stall,' said Dad.

Aaargghh. Henry could have burst into tears. Wasn't it just his rotten luck to try to get locked in a toilet which had gaps on the sides? Henry didn't much fancy wriggling round on the cold floor. Sighing, he gave the stall door a tug and opened it.

Horrid Henry sat in silence for the rest of the trip. He was so depressed he didn't even protest when Peter demanded his turn on the right. Plus, he felt carsick.

Henry rolled down his window.

'Mum!' said Peter. 'I'm cold.'

Dad turned the heat on.

'Having the heat on makes me feel sick,' said Henry.

'I'm going to be sick!' whimpered Peter.

'I'm going to be sick,' whined Henry.

'But we're almost there,' screeched Mum. 'Can't you hold on until –'

Bleecccchh.

Peter threw up all over Mum.

Bleecccchh.

Henry threw up all over Dad.

The car pulled into the driveway.

Mum and Dad staggered out of the car to Polly's front door.

'We survived,' said Mum, mopping her dress.

'Thank God that's over,' said Dad, mopping his shirt.

Horrid Henry scuffed his feet sadly behind them. Despite all his hard work, he'd lost the battle. While Rude Ralph and Dizzy Dave and Jolly Josh were dashing about spraying each other with green goo later this afternoon he'd be

stuck at a boring party with lots of grown-ups yak yak
yakking. Oh misery!

Ding dong.

The door opened. It was Prissy Polly. She was in
her bathrobe and slippers. She carried a stinky, smelly,
wailing baby over her shoulder. Pimply Paul followed.

He was wearing a filthy T-shirt with sick down the
front.

'Eeeek,' squeaked Polly.

Mum tried to look as if she had not been through
hell and barely lived to tell the tale.

'We're here!' said Mum brightly. 'How's the lovely baby?'

'Too prissy,' said Polly.

'Too pimply,' said Paul.

Polly and Paul looked at Mum and Dad.

'What are you doing here?' said Polly finally.

'We're here for the christening,' said Mum.

'Vera's christening?' said Polly.

'It's *next* weekend,' said Paul.

Mum looked like she wanted to sag to the floor.

Dad looked like he wanted to sag beside her.

'We've come on the wrong day?' whispered Mum.

'You mean, we have to go and come back?' whispered Dad.

'Yes,' said Polly.

'Oh no,' said Mum.

'Oh no,' said Dad.

'Bleecccch,' vomited Vera.

'Eeeek!' wailed Polly. 'Gotta go.'

She slammed the door.

'You mean, we can go home?' said Henry. 'Now?'

'Yes,' whispered Mum.

'Whoopee!' screamed Henry. 'Hang on, Ralph, here I come!'

Top tips to torment fellow passengers

1. Breathe loudly.
2. If there are three or more children, fight to get a window seat. If there are two children, fight to sit behind the driver so you can watch the speedometer.
3. Hum.
4. Ask 'Are we there yet?' every 30 seconds.
5. Get carsick.

Sharp prongs for teachers

statue of me

ordinary T.V. aerial

Satellite dish

video games

6. Make sure you take up as much room as possible. Steal as much space from your brother and sister as you can.
7. Demand lots of loo stops.
8. Fight about every CD. You only want the one someone else is listening to.
9. Get crumbs everywhere.
10. Fall asleep the moment you arrive.

jacuzzi

Boot full of toys

Spare toys

Spare food, (mainly sweets)

chocolate fountain

HORRiD HENRY'S DREAM CAR

HORRiD HENRY RUNS AWAY

Horrid Henry was not having a good day. His younger brother, Perfect Peter, had grabbed the hammock first and wouldn't get out. Then Mum had ordered him to tidy his room just when he was watching *Rapper Zapper* on TV. And now Dad was yelling at him.

'What's the meaning of this letter, Henry?' shouted Dad.

'What letter?' snapped Henry. He was sick and tired of being nagged at.

'You know perfectly well what letter!' said Mum. 'The letter from Miss Battle-Axe. The third this week.'

Oh, *that* letter.

Dear Henry's Parents,
I am sorry to tell you that today Henry:
Poked William
Tripped Linda
Shoved Dave
Pinched Andrew
Made rude noises, chewed gum, and would not stop talking in class
Yours Sincerely
Boudicca Battle-Axe

Henry scowled.

'Can I help it if I have to burp?'

'And what about all the children you hurt?' said Dad.

'I hardly touched William. Linda got in my way, and Dave and Andrew annoyed me,' said Henry. What a big fuss over nothing.

'Right,' said Dad. 'I am very disappointed with you. No TV, no comics and no sweets for a week.'

'A WEEK!' screamed Henry. 'For giving someone a little tap? It's not fair!'

'What about *my* letter?' said Peter.

Dear Peter's Parents
I am delighted to tell you that today Peter:
Helped Gordon
Shared with Sam
Volunteered to clean the paint-brushes, picked up the balls in P.E. and tidied the classroom without being asked.
Well done, Peter!
He is in the Good as Gold Book for the third time this month — a school record.
Yours Sincerely
Lydia Lovely

Dad glowed. 'At least *one* child in this family knows how to behave.'

Peter smiled modestly.

'You really should think more about other people, Henry,' said Peter. 'Then maybe one day *you'll* be in the Good as Gold Book.'

Horrid Henry snarled and leapt on Peter. He was primordial slime oozing over a trapped insect.

'Yeowww!' howled Peter.

'Stop it, Henry!' shouted Mum. 'Go straight to your room. NOW!'

Horrid Henry stomped upstairs to his bedroom and slammed the door.

'That's it!' screamed Henry. 'No one in this family likes me so I'm leaving!'

He'd show his horrible parents. He would run away to the jungle. He would fight giant snakes, crush crocodiles and paddle alone up piranha-infested rivers, hacking

his way through the vines. And he'd never ever come back. Then they'd be sorry. Serve them right for being so mean to him.

He could see them now. 'If only we'd been nicer to Henry', Dad would cry. 'Yes, such a lovely boy,' Mum would sob. 'Why oh why were we so cruel to him? If only Henry would come home he could always have the hammock,' Peter would whimper. 'Why was I so selfish?'

Shame really, thought Henry, dragging his suitcase from under the bed, that I won't be here to see them all wailing and gnashing their teeth.

Right, he thought, I'll only pack things I absolutely need. Lean and mean was the motto of Heroic Henry, Jungle Explorer.

Henry surveyed his room. What couldn't he live without?

He couldn't leave his Grisly Grub box and Dungeon Drink kit. Into the bag went the box and the kit. His Super Soaker 2000 water blaster would definitely come in handy in the wild. And of course, lots of games in case he got bored fighting panthers.

Comics? Henry considered … definitely. He stuffed a big stack in his bag. A few packets of crisps and some sweets would be good. And the box of Day-Glo slime. Henry certainly didn't want Peter getting his sticky fingers on his precious slime. Mr Kill? Nah! Mr Kill wouldn't be any use where he was going.

Perfect, thought Henry. Then he closed the bulging case. It would not shut. Very reluctantly Henry took out one comic and his football. There, he thought. He'd be off at dawn. And wouldn't they be sorry.

Tweet tweet.

Heroic Henry, Jungle Explorer, opened his eyes and leapt out of bed. The early birds were chirping. It was time to go. He flung on his jungle gear, then sneaked into Peter's room. He crept over to Peter's bed and pinched him.

'Wha-wha,' muttered Peter.

'Shut up and listen,' whispered Henry fiercely. 'I'm running away from home. If you tell anyone I've gone you'll be really sorry. In fact, you'll be dead.'

'I won't tell,' squeaked Peter.

'Good,' said Henry. 'And don't you dare touch anything in my room either.'

Horrid Henry crept down the stairs.

His suitcase clunked behind him. Henry froze. But no sound came from Mum and Dad's room.

35

At last Henry was safely down the stairs. Quietly he opened the back door and slipped into the misty garden.

He was outside. He was free! Goodbye civilization, thought Henry. Soon he'd be steaming down the Congo in search of adventure.

Of course I'll need a new name, thought Henry, as he began his long trek. To stop Mum and Dad tracking me down. Henry Intrepid sounded good. Piranha Pirate also had a nice ring. And I'll need to disguise myself too, thought Henry. He'd wait until he got to the jungle for that. He stole a quick glance behind him. No search party was after him so far.

Henry walked, and walked, and walked. His suitcase got heavier, and heavier, and heavier.

Phew! Henry was getting a bit tired dragging that case.

I feel like I've been travelling for miles, thought Henry. I think I'll stop and have a little rest at that secret hideaway. No one will find me there.

Horrid Henry clambered into the treehouse and stepped on something squishy.

'**AHHH!**' screamed Henry.

'**AHHH!**' screamed the Squishy Thing.

'What are *you* doing here?' snapped Horrid Henry.

'What are *you* doing here?' snapped Moody Margaret.

'I've run away from home, if you must know,' said Henry.

'So have I, and this is *my* treehouse,' said Margaret. 'Go away.'

'I can sit here if I want to,' said Henry, sitting down on Margaret's sleeping bag.

'Ouch! Get off my leg,' said Margaret, pushing him off.

'And don't think for a minute I'll let you come with me,' said Henry.

'You can't come with me, either,' said Margaret. 'So where are *you* going?'

'The Congo,' said Henry. He didn't know for sure exactly where that was, but he'd find it.

'Yuck,' said Margaret. 'Who'd want to go *there*? I'm going somewhere *much* better.'

'Where, smarty pants?' asked Henry. He eyed Margaret's rather plentiful stash of biscuits.

'Susan's house,' said Margaret.

Henry snorted.

'Susan's house? That's not running away.'

'It is too,' said Margaret.

''Tisn't.'

''Tis.'

''Tisn't.'

''Tis. And I slept here all night,' said Margaret.
'Where did *you* sleep?'

Henry eyed the distance between himself and
Margaret's biscuits. Whistling nonchalantly, Henry
stared in the opposite direction. Then, quick as a flash –
SNATCH!

Henry grabbed a handful of biscuits and stuffed
them in his mouth.

'Hey, that's my running-away food,' said Margaret.

'Not any more,' said Henry, snickering.

'Right,' said Margaret. She grabbed his case and
opened it. Then she hooted with laughter.

'That's all the food you brought?' she sneered. 'I'd like to see you get to the jungle with that. And all those comics! I bet you didn't even bring a map.'

'Oh yeah,' said Henry. 'What did *you* bring?'

Margaret opened her suitcase. Henry snorted with laughter.

'Clothes! I don't need clothes in the jungle. And anyway, *I* thought of running away first,' jeered Henry.

'Didn't,' said Margaret.

'Did,' said Henry.

'I'm going to tell your mother where you are,' said Margaret, 'and then you'll be in big trouble.'

'If you dare,' said Henry, 'I'll … I'll go straight over and tell yours. And I'll tell her you slept here last night. Won't you be in trouble then? In fact I'll go and tell her right now.'

'I'll tell yours first,' said Margaret.

They stood up, glaring at each other.

A faint, familiar smell drifted into the treehouse. It smelled like someone cooking.

Henry sniffed.

'What's that smell?'

Margaret sniffed.

'Pancakes,' she said.

Pancakes! Only Henry's favourite breakfast.

'Whose house?'

Margaret sniffed again.

'Yours,' she said sadly.

Yummy! Dad usually only made pancakes on special occasions. What could be happening? Then Henry had a terrible thought. Could it be … they were *celebrating* his departure?

How dare they? Well, he'd soon put a stop to that.

Henry clambered out of the treehouse and ran home.

'Mum! Dad! I'm back!' he shouted. 'Where are my pancakes?'

'They're all gone,' said Mum.

All gone!

'Why didn't you call me?' said Henry. 'You know I love pancakes.'

'We did call you,' said Mum, 'but you didn't come down. We thought you didn't want any.'

'But I wasn't here,' wailed Henry. He glared at Peter. Perfect Peter went on eating his pancakes a little faster, his arm protecting his plate.

'Peter knew I wasn't here,' said Henry. Then he lunged for Peter's plate. Peter screamed and held on tight.

'Henry said he'd kill me if I told so I didn't,' shrieked Peter.

'Henry, let go of that plate and don't be so horrid to your brother!' said Dad.

Henry let go. There was only half a pancake left anyway and it had Peter's yucky germs all over it.

Dad sighed.

'All right, I'll make another batch,' he said, getting up.

Henry was very surprised.

'Thanks, Dad,' said Henry. He sat down at the table.

A big steaming stack of pancakes arrived. Henry poured lashings of maple syrup on top, then stuffed a huge forkful of buttery pancakes into his mouth.

Yummy!

He'd head for the Congo tomorrow.

HEROIC HENRY, JUNGLE EXPLORER

Dear Horrible parents
That's it, I'm running away
to the jungle. Don't try to find
me, I will be far ~~away~~ too busy
fighting off snakes and
escaping from piranhas - if
I'm lucky. If you don't hear
from me it's because I've been
eaten by a crocodile, and
that will be all **YOUR** fault
for being so mean to me.
Henry

HORRID HENRY EATS A VEGETABLE

'Ugggh! Gross! Yuck! Bleeeeeech!'

Horrid Henry glared at the horrible, disgusting food slithering on his plate. Globby slobby blobs. Bumpy lumps. Rubbery blubbery globules of glop.

Ugggh!

How Dad and Mum and Peter could eat this swill without throwing up was amazing. Henry poked at the white, knobbly clump. It looked like brains. It felt like brains. Maybe it was . . .

Ewwwwwwww.

Horrid Henry pushed away his plate.

'I can't eat this,' moaned Henry. 'I'll be sick!'

'Henry! Cauliflower cheese is delicious,' said Mum.

'And nutritious,' said Dad.

'I love it,' said Perfect Peter. 'Can I have seconds?'

48

'It's nice to know *someone* appreciates my cooking,' said Dad. He frowned at Henry.

'But I hate vegetables,' said Henry. Yuck. Vegetables were so . . . healthy. And tasted so . . . vegetably. 'I want pizza!'

'Well, you can't have it,' said Dad.

'Ralph has pizza and chips every night at *his* house,' said Henry. 'And Graham *never* has to eat vegetables.'

'I don't care what Ralph and Graham eat,' said Mum.

'You've got to eat more vegetables,' said Dad.

'I eat loads of vegetables,' said Henry.

'Name one,' said Dad.

'Crisps,' said Henry.

'Crisps aren't vegetables, are they, Mum?' said Perfect Peter.

'No,' said Mum. 'Go on, Henry.'

'Ketchup,' said Henry.

'Ketchup is not a vegetable,' said Dad.

'It's impossible cooking for you,' said Mum.

'You're such a picky eater,' said Dad.

'I eat loads of things,' said Henry.

'Like what?' said Dad.

'Chips. Crisps. Burgers. Pizza. Chocolate. Sweets. Cake. Biscuits. Loads of food,' said Horrid Henry.

'That's not very healthy, Henry,' said Perfect Peter. 'You haven't said any fruit or vegetables.'

'So?' said Henry. 'Mind your own business, Toad.'

'Henry called me Toad,' wailed Peter.

'Ribbet. Ribbet,' croaked Horrid Henry.

'Don't be horrid, Henry,' snapped Dad.

'You can't go on eating so unhealthily,' said Mum.

'Agreed,' said Dad.

Uh oh, thought Henry. Here it comes. Nag nag nag. If there were prizes for best naggers Mum and Dad would win every time.

'I'll make a deal with you, Henry,' said Mum.

'What?' said Henry suspiciously. Mum and Dad's 'deals' usually involved his doing something horrible, for a pathetic reward. Well no way was he falling for that again.

'If you eat all your vegetables for five nights in a row, we'll take you to Gobble and Go.'

Henry's heart missed a beat. Gobble and Go! Gobble and Go! Only Henry's favourite restaurant in the whole wide world. Their motto: 'The chips just keep on coming!' shone forth from a purple neon sign. Music blared from twenty loudspeakers. Each table had its own TV. You could watch the chefs heat up your food in a giant microwave. Best of all, grown-ups never wanted to hang about for hours and chat. You ordered, gobbled, and left. Heaven.

And what fantastic food! Jumbo burgers. Huge pizzas. Lakes of ketchup. As many chips as you could eat. Fifty-two different ice creams. And not a vegetable in sight.

For some reason Mum and Dad hated Gobble and Go. They'd taken him once, and sworn they would never go again.

And now, unbelievably, Mum was offering.

'Deal!' shouted Henry, in case she changed her mind.

'So we're agreed,' said Mum. 'You eat your vegetables every night for five nights, and then we'll go.'

'Sure. Whatever,' said Horrid Henry eagerly. He'd agree to anything for a meal at Gobble and Go. He'd agree to dance naked down the street singing 'Hallelujah! I'm a nudie!' for the chance to eat at Gobble and Go.

52

Perfect Peter stopped eating his cauliflower. He didn't look very happy.

'I always eat *my* vegetables,' said Peter. 'What's my reward?'

'Health,' said Mum.

 **String beans.**

'Mum, Henry hasn't eaten any beans yet,' said Peter.

'I have too,' lied Henry.

'No you haven't,' said Peter. 'I've been watching.'

'Shut up, Peter,' said Henry.

'Mum!' wailed Peter. 'Henry told me to shut up.'

'Don't tell your brother to shut up,' said Mum.

'It's rude,' said Dad. 'Now eat your veg.'

Horrid Henry glared at his plate, teeming with slimy string beans. Just like a bunch of green worms, he thought. Yuck.

He must have been mad agreeing to eat vegetables for five nights in a row. He'd be poisoned before day three. Then they'd be sorry. 'How could we have been so cruel?' Mum would shriek. 'We've killed our own son,' Dad would moan. 'Why oh why did we make him eat his greens?' they would sob.

Too bad he'd be dead so he couldn't scream, 'I told you so!'

'We have a deal, Henry,' said Dad.

'I know,' snapped Henry.

He cut off the teeniest, tiniest bit of string bean he could.

'Go on,' said Mum.

Slowly, Horrid Henry lifted his fork and put the poison in his mouth.

Aaaarrrgggghhhhhh! What a horrible taste!

Henry spat and spluttered as the sickening sliver of string bean stuck in his throat.

'Water!' he gasped.

Perfect Peter speared several beans and popped them in his mouth.

'Great string beans, Dad,' said Peter. 'So crispy and crunchy.'

'Have mine if you like them so much,' muttered Henry.

'I want to see you eat every one of those string beans,' said Dad. 'Or no Gobble and Go.'

Horrid Henry scowled. No way was he eating another mouthful. The taste was too horrible. But, oh,

Gobble and Go. Those burgers! Those chips! Those TVs!

There had to be another way. Surely he, King Henry the Horrible, could defeat a plate of greens?

Horrid Henry worked out his battle plan. It was dangerous. It was risky. But what choice did he have?

First, he had to distract the enemy.

'You know, Mum,' said Henry, pretending to chew, 'you were right. These beans *are* very tasty.'

Mum beamed.

Dad beamed.

'I told you you'd like them if you tried them,' said Mum.

Henry pretended to swallow, then speared another bean. He pushed it round his plate.

Mum got up to refill the water jug. Dad turned to speak to her. Now was his chance!

Horrid Henry stretched out his foot under the table and lightly tickled Peter's leg.

'Look out, Peter, there's a spider on your leg.'

'Where?' squealed Peter, looking frantically under the table.

Leap! Plop!

Henry's beans hopped onto Peter's plate.

Peter raised his head.

'I don't see any spider,' said Peter.

'I knocked it off,' mumbled Henry, pretending to chew vigorously.

Then Peter saw his plate, piled high with string beans.

'Ooh,' said Peter, 'lucky me! I thought I'd finished!'

Tee hee, thought Horrid Henry.

Day 2 — Broccoli.

Plip!

A piece of Henry's broccoli 'accidentally' fell on the floor. Henry kicked it under Peter's chair.

Plop! Another piece of Henry's broccoli fell. And another. And another.

Plip plop. Plip plop. Plip plop.

Soon the floor under Peter's chair was littered with broccoli bits.

'Mum!' said Henry. 'Peter's making a mess.'

'Don't be a telltale, Henry,' said Dad.

'He's always telling on *me*,' said Henry.

Dad checked under Peter's chair.

'Peter! Eat more carefully. You're not a baby any more.'

Ha ha ha, thought Horrid Henry.

Day 3 — Peas.

Squish!

Henry flattened a pea under his knife.

57

Squash!

Henry flattened another one.

Squish. **Squash.** Squish. **Squash.**

Soon every pea was safely squished and hidden under Henry's knife.

'Great dinner, Dad,' said Horrid Henry. 'Especially the peas. I'll clear,' he added, carrying his plate to the sink and quickly rinsing his knife.

Dad beamed.

'Eating vegetables is making you helpful,' said Dad.

'Yes,' said Henry sweetly. 'It's great being helpful.'

Day 4 Cabbage.

Buzz. Buzzzzz.

'A fly landed on my cabbage!' shrieked Henry. He swatted the air with his hands. 'Where?' said Mum.

'There!' said Henry. He leapt out of his seat. 'Now it's on the fridge!'

'Buzz,' said Henry under his breath.

'I don't see any fly,' said Dad.

'Up there!' said Henry, pointing to the ceiling.

Mum looked up.

Dad looked up.

Peter looked up.

Henry dumped a handful of cabbage in the bin. Then he sat back down at the table.

'Rats,' said Henry. 'I can't eat the rest of my cabbage now, can I? Not after a filthy horrible disgusting fly has walked all over it, spreading germs and dirt and poo and—'

'All right all right,' said Dad. 'Leave the rest.'

I am a genius, thought Horrid Henry, smirking. Only one more battle until – Vegetable Victory!

Day 5 Sprouts.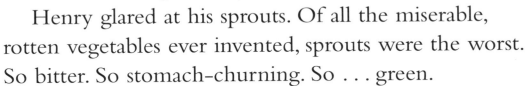

Mum ate her sprouts.

Dad ate his sprouts.

Peter ate his sprouts.

Henry glared at his sprouts. Of all the miserable, rotten vegetables ever invented, sprouts were the worst. So bitter. So stomach-churning. So . . . green.

But how to get rid of them? There was Peter's head, a tempting target. A very tempting target. Henry's sprout-flicking fingers itched. No, thought Horrid Henry. I can't blow it when I'm so close.

Should he throw them on the floor? Spit them in his napkin?

Or – Horrid Henry beamed. There was a little drawer in the table in front of Henry's chair. A perfect, Brussels sprout-sized drawer.

Henry eased it open. What could be simpler than stuffing a sprout or two inside while pretending to eat?

Soon the drawer was full. Henry's plate was empty.

'Look Mum! Look Dad!' screeched Henry. 'All gone!' Which was true, he thought gleefully.

'Well done, Henry,' said Dad.

'Well done, Henry,' said Peter.

'We'll take you to Gobble and Go tomorrow,' said Mum.

'Yippee!' screamed Horrid Henry.

Mum, Dad, Henry, and Peter walked up the street.

Mum, Dad, Henry, and Peter walked down the street.

Where was Gobble and Go, with its flashing neon sign, blaring music, and purple walls? They must have walked past it.

But how? Horrid Henry looked about wildly. It was impossible to miss Gobble and Go. You could see that neon sign for miles.

'It was right here,' said Horrid Henry.

But Gobble and Go was gone.

A new restaurant squatted in its place.

'The Virtuous Veggie,' read the sign. 'The all new vegetable restaurant!'

Horrid Henry gazed in horror at the menu posted outside.

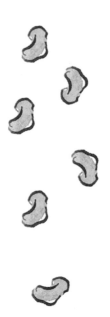

Cabbage Casserole
Pop-up Peas
Spinach Surprise
Sprouts a go-go
Choice of rhubarb or
broccoli ice cream

'Yummy!' said Perfect Peter.

'Look, Henry,' said Mum. 'It's serving all your new favourite vegetables.'

Horrid Henry opened his mouth to protest. Then he closed it. He knew when he was beaten.

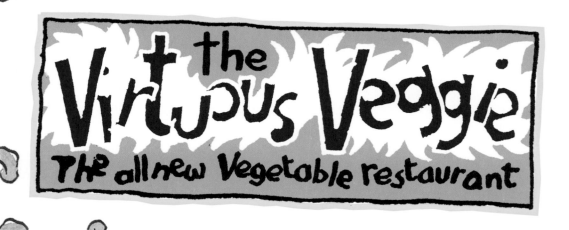

DANGER!
POISON!
TOXIC!
KILLER VEG

Do not eat on pain of death

I WANT!
GIMME!
BOY!
BOY!
BOY!

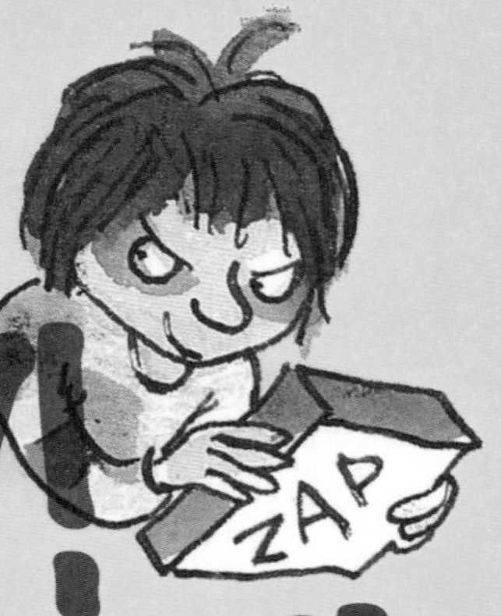

HORRID HENRY GOES SHOPPING

Horrid Henry stood in his bedroom up to his knees in clothes. The long sleeve stripy T-shirt came to his elbow. His trousers stopped halfway down his legs. Henry sucked in his tummy as hard as he could. Still the zip wouldn't zip.

'Nothing fits!' he screamed, yanking off the shirt and hurling it across the room. 'And my shoes hurt.'

'All right Henry, calm down,' said Mum. 'You've grown. We'll go out this afternoon and get you some new clothes and shoes.'

'**NOOOOOO!**' shrieked Henry.

'**NOOOOOOOOOOOOO!**'

Horrid Henry hated shopping.

Correction: Horrid Henry loved shopping. He loved shopping for gigantic TVs, computer games, comics, toys, and sweets. Yet for some reason Horrid Henry's parents never wanted to go shopping for good stuff. Oh no. They shopped for hoover bags. Toothpaste. Spinach. Socks. Why oh why did he have such horrible parents? When he was grown-up he'd never set foot in

a supermarket. He'd only shop for TVs, computer games, and chocolate.

But shopping for clothes was even worse than heaving his heavy bones round the Happy Shopper Supermarket. Nothing was more boring than being dragged round miles and miles and miles of shops, filled with disgusting clothes only a mutant would ever want to wear, and then standing in a little room while Mum made you try on icky scratchy things you wouldn't be seen dead in if they were the last trousers on earth. It was horrible enough getting dressed once a day without doing it fifty times. Just thinking about trying on shirt after shirt after shirt made Horrid Henry want to scream.

'I'm not going shopping!' he howled, kicking the pile of clothes as viciously as he could. 'And you can't make me.'

'What's all this yelling?' demanded Dad.

'Henry needs new trousers,' said Mum grimly.

Dad went pale.

'Are you sure?'

'Yes,' said Mum. 'Take a look at him.'

Dad looked at Henry. Henry scowled.

'They're a *little* small, but not *that* bad,' said Dad.

'I can't breathe in these trousers!' shrieked Henry.

'That's why we're going shopping,' said Mum. 'And *I'll* take him.' Last time Dad had taken Henry shopping for socks and came back instead with three Hairy Hellhound CDs and a jumbo pack of Day-Glo slime.

'I don't know what came over me,' Dad had said, when Mum told him off.

'But why do *I* have to go?' said Henry. 'I don't want to waste my precious time shopping.'

'What about *my* precious time?' said Mum.

Henry scowled. Parents didn't have precious time. They were there to serve their children. New trousers should just magically appear, like clean clothes and packed lunches.

Mum's face brightened. 'Wait, I have an idea,' she beamed. She rushed out and came back with a large plastic bag. 'Here,' she said, pulling out a pair of bright red trousers, 'try these on.'

Henry looked at them suspiciously.

'Where are they from?'

'Aunt Ruby dropped off some of Steve's old clothes a few weeks ago. I'm sure we'll find something that fits you.'

Horrid Henry stared at Mum. Had she gone gaga? Was she actually suggesting that he should wear his horrible cousin's mouldy old shirts and pongy pants? Just imagine, putting his arms into the same stinky sleeves that Stuck-up Steve had slimed? Uggh!

'NO WAY!' screamed Henry, shuddering. 'I'm not wearing Steve's smelly old clothes. I'd catch rabies.'

'They're practically brand new,' said Mum.

'I don't care,' said Henry.

'But Henry,' said Perfect Peter. 'I always wear *your* hand-me-downs.'

'So?' snarled Henry.

'I don't mind wearing hand-me-downs,' said Perfect Peter. 'It saves so much money. You shouldn't be so selfish, Henry.'

'Quite right, Peter,' said Mum, smiling. 'At least *one* of my sons thinks about others.'

Horrid Henry pounced. He was a vampire sampling his supper.

'AAIIIEEEEEE!' squealed Peter.

'Stop that, Henry!' screamed Mum.

'Leave your brother alone!' screamed Dad.

Horrid Henry glared at Peter.

'Peter is a worm, Peter is a toad,' jeered Henry.

'Mum!' wailed Peter. 'Henry said I was a worm. And a toad.'

'Don't be horrid, Henry,' said Dad. 'Or no TV for a week. You have three choices. Wear Steve's old clothes. Wear your old clothes. Go shopping for new ones today.'

'Do we *have* to go today?' moaned Henry.

'Fine,' said Mum. 'We'll go tomorrow.'

'I don't want to go tomorrow,' wailed Henry. 'My weekend will be ruined.'

Mum glared at Henry.

'Then we'll go right now this minute.'

NO!' screamed Horrid Henry.

YES!' screamed Mum.

Several hours later, Mum and Henry walked into Mellow Mall. Mum already looked like she'd been crossing the Sahara desert without water for days. Serve her right for bringing me here, thought

Horrid Henry, scowling, as he scuffed his feet.

'Can't we go to Shop 'n' Drop?' whined Henry. 'Graham says they've got a win your weight in chocolate competition.'

'No,' said Mum, dragging Henry into Zippy's Department Store. 'We're here to get you some new trousers and shoes. Now hurry up, we don't have all day.'

Horrid Henry looked around. Wow! There was lots of great stuff on display.

'I want the Hip-Hop Robots,' said Henry.

'No,' said Mum.

'I want the new Supersoaker!' screeched Henry.

'No,' said Mum.

'I want a Creepy Crawly lunchbox!'

'NO!' said Mum, pulling him into the boys' clothing department.

What, thought Horrid Henry grimly, is the point of going shopping if you never buy anything?

'I want Root-a-Toot trainers with flashing red lights,' said Henry. He could see himself now, strolling into class, a bugle blasting and red light flashing every time his feet hit the floor. Cool! He'd love to see Miss Battle-Axe's face when he exploded into class wearing them.

'No,' said Mum, shuddering.

'Oh please,' said Henry.

'NO!' said Mum, 'we're here to buy trousers and sensible school shoes.'

'But I want Root-a-Toot trainers!' screamed Horrid Henry. 'Why can't we buy what *I* want to buy? You're the meanest mother in the world and I hate you!'

'Don't be horrid, Henry. Go and try these on,' said Mum, grabbing a selection of hideous trousers and revolting T-shirts. 'I'll keep looking.'

Horrid Henry sighed loudly and slumped towards the dressing room. No one in the world suffered as much as he did. Maybe he could hide between the clothes racks and never come out.

Then something wonderful in the toy department next door caught his eye.

Whooa! A whole row of the new megalotronic animobotic robots with 213 programmable actions. Horrid Henry dumped the clothes and ran over to have a look. Oooh, the new Intergalactic Samurai Gorillas which launched real stinkbombs! And the latest Super Soakers! And deluxe Dungeon Drink kits with a celebrity chef recipe book! To say nothing of the Mega–Whirl Goo-Shooter which sprayed fluorescent goo for fifty metres in every direction. Wow!

Mum staggered into the dressing room with more clothes. 'Henry?' said Mum.

No reply.

'HENRY!' said Mum.

Still no reply.

Mum yanked open a dressing room door.

'Hen—'

'Excuse *me!*' yelped a bald man, standing in his underpants.

'Sorry,' said Mum, blushing bright pink. She dashed out of the changing room and scanned the shop floor.

Henry was gone.

Mum searched up the aisles.

No Henry.

Mum searched down the aisles.

Still no Henry.

Then Mum saw a tuft of hair sticking up behind the neon sign for Ballistic Bazooka Boomerangs. She marched over and hauled Henry away.

'I was just looking,' protested Henry.

Henry tried on one pair of trousers after another.

'No, no, no, no, no, no, no,' said Henry, kicking off the final pair. 'I hate all of them.'

'All right,' said Mum, grimly. 'We'll look somewhere else.'

Mum and Henry went to Top Trousers. They went to Cool Clothes. They went to Stomp in the Swamp. Nothing had been right.

'Too tight,' moaned Henry.

'Too itchy!'

'Too big!'

'Too small!'

'Too ugly!'

'Too red!'

'Too uncomfortable!'

'We're going to Tip-Top Togs,' said Mum wearily. 'The first thing that fits, we're buying.'

Mum staggered into the children's department and grabbed a pair of pink and green tartan trousers in Henry's size.

'Try these on,' she ordered. 'If they fit we're having them.'

Horrid Henry gazed in horror at the horrendous trousers.

'Those are girls' trousers!' he screamed.

'They are not,' said Mum.

'Are too!' shrieked Henry.

'I'm sick and tired of your excuses, Henry,' said Mum. 'Put them on or no pocket money for a year. I mean it.'

Horrid Henry put on the pink and green tartan trousers, puffing out his stomach as much as possible. Not even Mum would make him buy trousers that were too tight.

Oh no. The horrible trousers had an elastic waist. They would fit a mouse as easily as an elephant.

'And lots of room to grow,' said Mum brightly. 'You can wear them for years. Perfect.'

'NOOOOOOO!'

howled Henry. He flung himself on the floor kicking and screaming.

'NOOOOOOO!'
'They're GIRLS' trousers!!!'

'We're buying them,' said Mum. She gathered up the tartan trousers and stomped over to the till. She tried not to think about starting all over again trying to find a pair of shoes that Henry would wear.

A little girl in pigtails walked out of the dressing room, twirling in pink and green tartan trousers.

'I love them, Mummy!' she shrieked. 'Let's get three pairs.'

Horrid Henry stopped howling. He looked at Mum.

Mum looked at Henry.

Then they both looked at the pink and green tartan trousers Mum was carrying.

ROOT-A-TOOT!
ROOT-A-TOOT!
ROOT-A-TOOT!
TOOT! TOOT!

An earsplitting bugle blast shook the house. Flashing
red lights bounced off the walls.

'What's that noise?' said Dad, covering his ears.

'What noise?' said Mum, pretending to read.

ROOT-A-TOOT!
ROOT-A-TOOT!
ROOT-A-TOOT!
TOOT! TOOT!

Dad stared at Mum.

'You didn't,' said Dad. 'Not—Root-a-Toot trainers?'

Mum hid her face in her hands.

'I don't know what came over me,' said Mum.

HORRID HENRY'S SHOPPING LIST

What I need !!!!!!!!

10 pairs of Root-a-Toot trainers

Megalotronic Animobotic Robots
(plus attachments)

Creepy-Crawly lunchbox
and flask

Hairy Hellhound Greatest Hits

Mega-gigantic TV with
wraparound screen and
12 speakers

HORRID HENRY'S HOBBY

'Out of my way, worm!' shrieked Horrid Henry, pushing past his younger brother Perfect Peter and dashing into the kitchen.

'NO!' screamed Perfect Peter. He scrambled after Henry and clutched his leg.

'Get off me!' shouted Henry. He grabbed the unopened Sweet Tweet cereal box. 'Nah nah ne nah nah, I got it first.'

Perfect Peter lunged for the Sweet Tweet box and snatched it from Henry. 'But it's my turn!'

'No, mine!' shrieked Henry. He ripped open the top and stuck his hand inside.

'It's mine!' shrieked Peter. He ripped open the bottom.

A small wrapped toy fell to the floor.

Henry and Peter both lunged for it.

'Gimme that!' yelled Henry.

'But it's my turn to have it!' yelled Peter.

'Stop being horrid, Henry!' shouted Mum. 'Now give me that thing!'

Henry and Peter both held on tight.

'NO!' screamed Henry and Peter. 'IT'S MY TURN TO HAVE THE TOY!'

Horrid Henry and Perfect Peter both collected Gizmos from inside Sweet Tweet cereal boxes. So did everyone at their school. There were ten different coloured Gizmos to collect, from the common green to the rare gold. Both Henry and Peter had Gizmos of every colour. Except for one. Gold.

'Right,' said Mum, 'whose turn is it to get the toy?'

'MINE!' screamed Henry and Peter.

'He got the last one!' screeched Henry. 'Remember – he opened the new box and got the blue Gizmo.'

It was true that Perfect Peter had got the blue Gizmo – two boxes ago. But why should Peter get any? If he hadn't started collecting Gizmos to copy me, thought Henry resentfully, I'd get every single one.

'NO!' howled Peter. He burst into tears. 'Henry opened the last box.'

'Crybaby,' jeered Henry.

'Stop it,' said Peter.

'Stop it,' mimicked Henry.

'Mum, Henry's teasing me,' wailed Peter.

'I remember now,' said Mum. 'It's Peter's turn.'

'Thank you, Mum,' said Perfect Peter.

'It's not fair!' screamed Horrid Henry as Peter tore open the wrapping. There was a gold gleam.

'Oh my goodness,' gasped Peter. 'A gold Gizmo!'

Horrid Henry felt as if he'd been punched in the stomach. He stared at the glorious, glowing, golden Gizmo.

'It's not fair!' howled Henry. 'I want a gold Gizmo!'

'I'm sorry, Henry,' said Mum. 'It'll be your turn next.'

'But I want the gold one!' screamed Henry.

He leaped on Peter and yanked the Gizmo out of his hand. He was Hurricane Henry uprooting everything in his path.

Helllllllp!'

howled Peter.

'Stop being horrid, Henry, or no more Gizmos for you!' shouted Mum. 'Now clean up this mess and get dressed.'

'NO!' howled Henry. He ran upstairs to his room, slamming the door behind him.

He had to have a gold Gizmo. He simply had to. No one at school had a gold one. Henry could see himself now, the centre of attention, everyone pushing and shoving just to get a look at his gold Gizmo. Henry could charge 20p a peek. Everyone would want

to see it and to hold it. Henry would be invited to every birthday party. Instead, Peter would be the star attraction. Henry gnashed his teeth just thinking about it.

But how could he get one? You couldn't buy Gizmos. You could only get them inside Sweet Tweet cereal boxes. Mum was so mean she made Henry and

Peter finish the old box before she'd buy a new one. Henry had eaten mountains of Sweet Tweet cereal to collect all his Gizmos. All that hard work would be in vain, unless he got a gold one.

He could, of course, steal Peter's. But Peter would be sure to notice, and Henry would be the chief suspect.

He could swap. Yes! He would offer Peter *two* greens! That was generous. In fact, that was really generous. But Peter hated doing swaps. For some reason he always thought Henry was trying to cheat him.

And then suddenly Henry had a brilliant, spectacular idea. True, it did involve a little tiny teensy weensy bit of trickery, but Henry's cause was just. *He'd* been collecting Gizmos far longer than Peter had. He deserved a gold one, and Peter didn't.

'So, you got a gold Gizmo,' said Henry, popping into Peter's room. 'I'm really sorry.'

Perfect Peter looked up from polishing his Gizmos. 'Why?' he said suspiciously. '*Everyone* wants a gold Gizmo.'

Horrid Henry looked sadly at Perfect Peter. 'Not any more. They're very unlucky, you know. Every single person who's got one has died horribly.'

Perfect Peter stared at Henry, then at his golden Gizmo.

'That's not true, Henry.'

'Yes it is.'

'No it isn't.'

Horrid Henry walked slowly around Peter's room. Every so often he made a little note in a notebook.

'Marbles, check. Three knights, check. Nature kit – nah. Coin collection, check.'

'What are you doing?' said Peter.

'Just looking round your stuff to see what I want when you're gone.'

'Stop it!' said Peter. 'You just made that up about gold Gizmos – didn't you?'

'No,' said Henry. 'It's in all the newspapers. There was the boy out walking his dog who fell into a pit of

90

molten lava. There was the girl who drowned in the loo, and then that poor boy who—'

'I don't want to die,' said Perfect Peter. He looked pale. 'What am I going to do?'

Henry paused. 'There's nothing you can do. Once you've got it you're sunk.'

Peter jumped up.

'I'll throw it away!'

'That wouldn't work,' said Henry. 'You'd still be jinxed. There's only one way out—'

'What?' said Perfect Peter.

'If you give the gold away to someone brave enough to take it, then the jinx passes to them.'

'But no one will take it from me!' wailed Peter.

'Tell you what,' said Henry. 'I'll take the risk.'

'Are you sure?' said Peter.

'Of course,' said Horrid Henry. 'You're my brother. You'd risk your life for me.'

'OK,' said Peter. He handed Henry the gold Gizmo. 'Thank you, Henry. You're the best brother in the world.'

'I know,' said Horrid Henry.

He actually had his very own gold Gizmo in his hand. It was his, fair and square. He couldn't wait to see Moody Margaret's face when he waved it in front of her. And Rude Ralph. He would be green with envy.

Then Perfect Peter burst into tears and ran downstairs.

'Mum!' he wailed. 'Henry's going to die! And it's all my fault.'

'What?' screeched Mum.

Uh oh, thought Henry. He clutched his treasure.

Mum stormed upstairs. She snatched the gold Gizmo from Henry.

'How could you be so horrid, Henry?' shouted Mum. 'No TV for a week! Poor Peter. Now get ready. We're going shopping.'

'NO!' howled Henry. 'I'm not going!'

Horrid Henry scowled as he followed Mum up and down the aisles of the Happy Shopper. He'd crashed the cart into some people so Mum wouldn't let him push it. Then she caught him filling the cart with crisps and fizzy drinks and made him put them all back. What a horrible rotten day this had turned out to be.

'Yum, cabbage,' said Perfect Peter. 'Could we get some?'

'Certainly,' said Mum.

'And sprouts, my favourite!' said Peter.

'Help yourself,' said Mum.

'I want sweets!' screamed Henry.

'No,' said Mum.

'I want doughnuts!' screamed Henry.

'No!' screamed Mum.

'There's nothing to eat here!' shrieked Henry.

'Stop being horrid, Henry,' hissed Mum. 'Everyone's looking.'

'I don't care.'

'Well I do,' said Mum. 'Now make yourself useful. Go and get a box of Sweet Tweets.'

'All right,' said Henry. Now was his chance to escape. Before Mum could stop him he grabbed a cart and whizzed off.

'Watch out for the racing driver!' squealed Henry.

Shoppers scattered as he zoomed down the aisle and screeched to a halt in front of the cereal section. There were the Sweet Tweets. A huge pile of them, in a display tower, under a twinkling sign saying, 'A free Gizmo in every box! Collect them all!'

Henry reached for a box and put it in his cart.

And then Horrid Henry stopped. What was the point of buying a whole box if it just contained another green Gizmo? Henry didn't think he could bear it. I'll just check what's inside, he thought. Then, if it *is* a green one, I'll be prepared for the disappointment.

Carefully, he opened the box and slipped his hand inside. Aha! There was the toy. He lifted it out, and held it up to the light. Rats! A green Gizmo, just what he'd feared.

But wait. There was bound to be a child out there longing for a green Gizmo to complete his collection just as much as Henry was longing for a gold. Wouldn't it be selfish and horrid of Henry to take a green he didn't need when it would make someone else so happy?

I'll just peek inside one more box, thought Horrid Henry, replacing the box he'd opened and reaching for another.

He tore it open. Red.

Hmmm, thought Henry. Red is surplus to requirements.

Another box opened. Blue.

Green! Green! Blue!

I'll just try one more at the back, thought Henry. He stood on tiptoe, and stretched as far as he could. His hand reached inside the box and grabbed hold of the toy.

The tower wobbled.

Horrid Henry sprawled on the ground. Henry was covered in Sweet Tweets. So was the floor. So were all the shoppers.

HELP!'

screamed the manager, skidding in the mess. 'Whose horrid boy is this?'

Skid!

There was a very long silence.
'Mine,' whispered Mum.

Horrid Henry sat in the kitchen surrounded by boxes and boxes and boxes of Sweet Tweets. He'd be eating Sweet Tweets for breakfast, lunch and dinner for weeks. But it was worth it, thought Henry happily.

Banned for life from the Happy Shopper, how wonderful. He uncurled his hand to enjoy again the glint of gold.

Although he *had* noticed that Scrummy Yummies were offering a free Twizzle card in every box. Hmmmm, Twizzle cards.

THE HENRY MUSEUM

HORRID HENRY'S BATHTIME

Horrid Henry loved baths.

He loved causing great big tidal waves.

He loved making bubble-bath beards and bubble-bath hats.

He loved staging battles with Yellow Duck and Snappy Croc. He loved diving for buried treasure, fighting sea monsters, and painting the walls with soapy suds.

But best of all, being in the bath meant Peter couldn't bother him, or wreck his games or get him into trouble.

Henry stretched out in the lovely warm water. The bubbles were piled high to overflowing, just as he liked.

A bucketload of soapy suds cascaded onto the floor. Yippee! The first tidal wave of the day. Good thing Mum wasn't around. But then what Mum didn't know wouldn't hurt her.

Now what to do first? A Croc and Duck fight? Or the killer tidal wave?

'Heh heh heh,' cackled Horrid Henry, 'watch your tail Yellow Duck, 'cause Snappy Croc is on the attack. Snap! Snap! Snap!'

Suddenly the bathroom door opened. A slimy toad slithered in.

'Oy, get out of here, Peter,' said Henry.

'Dad said we had to share a bath,' said Perfect Peter, taking off his shirt.

What?

'Liar!' screeched Horrid Henry. 'You are dead meat!' He reached for his Super Soaker. Henry was not allowed to use it in the house, but this was an emergency.

'AAARRRGGGHHH,' squealed Peter as a jet of water hit him in the face.

Dad dashed in.

'Put that Super Soaker away or I'll confiscate it,' shouted Dad.

Henry's finger trembled on the trigger. Dad's red face was so tempting . . .

Henry could see it now. POW! Dad soaking wet. Dad screaming. Dad snatching the Super Soaker and throwing it in the rubbish and telling Henry no TV for ever . . .

Hmmm. Dad's red face was a little less tempting.

'Just look at this floor, Henry,' said Dad. 'What a waste of water.'

'It's not a waste,' said Horrid Henry, holding tight onto his Super Soaker in case Dad lunged, 'it's a tidal wave.'

'Too much water is being wasted in this house,' said Dad. 'From now on you and Peter will share a bath.'

Horrid Henry could not believe his ears. *Share* a bath? *Share* a bath with stupid smelly Peter?

'NOOOO,' wailed Henry.

'I don't mind sharing, Dad,' said Peter. 'We all have to do our bit to save water.'

'But Peter pees in the bath,' said Henry.

'I do not,' said Perfect Peter. 'Henry does.'

'Liar!'

'Liar!'

'And we'll be squashed!' wailed Henry. 'And he likes the bath too cold ! And he – '

'That's enough Henry,' said Dad. 'Now make room for Peter.'

Horrid Henry ducked his head under water. He was never coming back up. Never. Then they'd be sorry they made him share his bath with an ugly toad snotface telltale goody-goody poo breath . . .

GASP.

Horrid Henry came up for air.

'If you don't make room for Peter you'll be getting out now,' said Dad. 'And no TV for a week.'

Scowling, Horrid Henry moved his legs a fraction of an inch.

'Henry . . .' said Dad.

Horrid Henry moved his legs another fraction.

'I don't want to sit by the taps,' said Peter. 'They hurt my back.'

'Well I don't want to sit there either,' said Henry. 'And I was here first. I'm not moving.'

'Just get in, Peter,' said Dad.

Perfect Peter got in the bath and sat against the taps. His lower lip trembled.

Ha ha ha, thought Horrid Henry, stretching out his

legs. Peter was all squished at the yucky end of the bath. Good. Serve him right for ruining Henry's fun.

'Nah nah ne nah nah,' chortled Horrid Henry.

'Dad, the bath's too hot,' moaned Peter. 'I'm boiling.'
Dad added cold water.

'Too cold!' screeched Horrid Henry. 'I'm freezing!'
Dad added hot water.

'Too hot!' said Perfect Peter.

Dad sighed.

'New house rule: the person who sits by the taps decides the temperature,' said Dad, letting in a trickle of cold water. 'Now I don't want to hear another peep out of either of you,' he added, closing the door.

Horrid Henry could have punched himself. Why hadn't he thought of that? If he were by the taps *he'd* be the bath king.

'Move,' said Henry.

'No,' said Peter.

'I want to sit by the taps,' said Henry.

'Too bad,' said Peter. 'I'm not moving.'

'Make it hotter,' ordered Henry.

'No,' said Peter. 'I control the temperature because *I'm* sitting by the taps.'

'DAD!' shouted Henry. 'Peter wants the bath too cold!'

'MUM!' shouted Peter. 'Henry wants the bath too hot!'

'I'm freezing!'

'I'm boiling!'

'Be quiet both of you,' screamed Dad from the kitchen.

Horrid Henry glared at Peter.

Perfect Peter glared at Henry.

'Move your legs,' said Henry.

'I'm on my side,' said Peter.

Henry kicked him.

'No you're not,' said Henry.

Peter kicked him back.

Henry splashed him.

'Muuuuuuum!' shrieked Peter. 'Henry's being horrid.'

'Peter's being horrid!'

'Make him stop!' shouted Henry and Peter.

'AAARRRGGGHHH!'

screeched Peter.

'AAARRRGGGHHH!'

screeched Henry.

'Stop fighting!' screamed Mum.

Perfect Peter picked up Yellow Duck.

'Give me Yellow Duck,' hissed Henry.

'No,' said Peter.

'But it's my duck!'

'Mine!'

'WAAAAAAA!'

wailed Peter. 'Muuuuuuuum!'

Mum ran in. 'What's going on in here?'

'He hit me!' screeched Henry and Peter.

'That's it, both of you out,' said Mum.

'Bathtime, boys,' said Mum the next evening.

Horrid Henry raced upstairs. This time he'd make sure he was the first one in. But when he reached the bathroom, a terrible sight met his eyes. There was Peter, already sitting at the tap end. Henry could practically see the ice cubes floating on the freezing water.

Rats. Another bathtime ruined.

Henry stuck his toe in.

'It's too cold!' moaned Henry. 'And I don't want to have a bath with Peter. I want my own bath.'

'Stop making a fuss and get in,' said Mum. 'And no fighting. I'm leaving the door open.'

Horrid Henry got into the bath.

Eeeeek! He was turning into an icicle! Well, not for

long. He had a brilliant, spectacular plan.

'Stop making ripples,' hissed Horrid Henry. 'You have to keep the water smooth.'

'I am keeping the water smooth,' said Peter.

'Shh! Hold still.'

'Why?' said Peter.

'I wouldn't splash if I were you,' whispered Henry. '*It* doesn't like splashing.'

'Why are you whispering?' said Peter.

'Because there's a monster in the tub,' said Henry.

'No there isn't,' said Peter.

'It's the plughole monster,' said Horrid Henry. 'It sneaks up the drains, slithers through the plughole and – slurp! Down you go.'

'You big liar,' said Peter. He shifted slightly off the plughole.

Henry shrugged.

'It's up to you,' he said. 'Don't say I didn't warn you when the Plughole Monster sucks you down the drain!'

Peter scooted away from the plughole.

'MUUUUM!' he howled, jumping out of the bath.

Henry grabbed his spot, turned on the hot water, and stretched out. Ahhhh!

Peter continued to shriek.

'What's going on in here?' said Mum and Dad, bursting into the bathroom.

'Henry said I was going to get sucked down the plughole,' snivelled Peter.

'Don't be horrid, Henry,' said Mum. 'Get out of the bath this minute.'

'But – but . . .' said Horrid Henry.

'New house rules,' said Mum. 'From now on *I'll* run the bath and *I'll* decide the temperature.'

We'll see about that, thought Horrid Henry.

The next evening, Henry sneaked into the bathroom. A thin trickle of water dribbled from the tap. The bath was just starting to fill. He felt the water.

Brrr! Freezing cold. Just how he hated it. Peter must have fiddled with the temperature. Well, no way! Henry turned up the hot tap full blast. Hot water gushed into the bath. That's much better, thought Horrid Henry. He smiled and went downstairs.

From his bedroom, Peter heard Henry stomping from the bathroom. What was he up to? When the coast was clear, Peter tiptoed into the bathroom and dipped his fingers in the water. Oww! Boiling hot. Just how he hated it. Henry must have fiddled with the temperature:

Mum would *never* make it so hot. Peter turned up the cold tap full blast. Much better, thought Peter.

Mum and Dad were sitting in the kitchen drinking tea.

Mum smiled. 'It's lovely and quiet upstairs, isn't it?'

Dad smiled. 'I knew they'd be able to share a bath, in the end.'

Mum stopped smiling.

'Do you hear something?'

Dad listened.

'Leave me alone!' screamed Henry from the sitting room.

'You leave me alone!' screamed Peter.

'Just the usual,' said Dad.

'Didn't you put them in the bath?'

Dad stopped smiling. 'No. Didn't you?'

Mum looked at Dad.

Dad looked at Mum.

Plink! Plink! Plink!

Water began to drip from the ceiling.

'I think I hear – RUNNING WATER!' screamed Mum. She dashed up the stairs.

Dad ran after her.

Mum opened the bathroom door.

Water gushed from the bathroom, and roared down the stairs.

Slip!

Slide!

Mum landed on her bottom.

Plop!

Dad toppled into the bath.

Splash!

'It wasn't me!' screamed Henry.

'It wasn't me!' wailed Peter. Then he burst into tears.

'Mum!' wept Peter. 'I've been a bad boy.'

Snap! Snap!

Snappy Croc was defending his tail. Yellow Duck was twisting round to attack. Ka-boom!

Horrid Henry lay back in the bath and closed his eyes. Mum and Dad had decided to let Henry have baths on his own. To save water, they'd take showers.

HORRID HENRY RULES THE WAVES

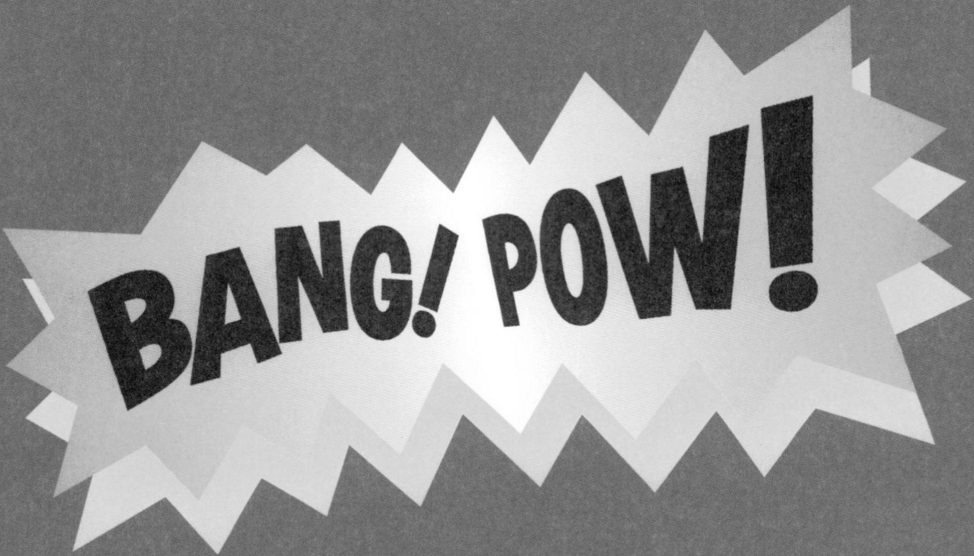
BANG! POW!

HORRiD HENRY AND THE MEGA-MEAN TIME MACHINE

orrid Henry flicked the switch. The time machine whirred. Dials spun. Buttons pulsed. Latches locked. Horrid Henry, Time Traveller, was ready for blast off!

Now, where to go, where to go?

Dinosaurs, thought Henry. Yes! Henry loved dinosaurs. He would love to stalk a few Tyrannosaurus Rexes as they rampaged through the primordial jungle.

But what about King Arthur and the Knights of the Round Table? 'Arise, Sir Henry,' King Arthur would say, booting Lancelot out of his chair. 'Sure thing, King,' Sir Henry would reply, twirling his sword. 'Out of my way, worms!'

Or what about the siege of Troy? Heroic Henry, that's who he'd be, the fearless fighter dashing about doing daring deeds.

Tempting, thought Henry. Very tempting.

Wait a sec, what about visiting the future, where school was banned and parents had to do whatever their children told them? Where everyone had their own spaceship and ate sweets for dinner. And where King Henry the Horrible ruled supreme, chopping off the head of anyone who dared to say no to him.

To the future, thought Henry, setting the dial.

Henry braced himself for the jolt into hyperspace —

'Henry, it's my turn.'
Horrid Henry ignored the alien's whine.

'Henry! If you don't share I'm going to tell Mum.'

AAAARRRRGGGHHHHHH.

The Time Machine juddered to a halt. Henry climbed out.

'Go away, Peter,' said Henry. 'You're spoiling everything.'

'But it's my turn.'

'GO AWAY!'

'Mum said we could *both* play with the box,' said Peter. 'We could cut out windows, make a little house, paint flowers – '

'NO!' screeched Henry.

'But . . . ' said Peter. He stood in the sitting room, holding his scissors and crayons.

'Don't you touch my box!' hissed Henry.

'I will if I want to,' said Peter. 'And it's not yours.' Henry had no right to boss him around, thought Peter. He'd been waiting such a long time for his turn.

Well, he wasn't waiting any longer. He'd start cutting out a window this minute.

Peter got out his scissors.

'Stop! It's a time machine, you toad!' shrieked Henry.

Peter paused.

Peter gasped.

Peter stared at the huge cardboard box. A time machine? *A time machine?* How could it be a time machine?

'It is not,' said Peter.

'Is too,' said Henry.

'But it's made of cardboard,' said Peter. 'And the washing machine came in it.'

Henry sighed.

'Don't you know anything? If it *looked* like a time machine everyone would try to steal it. It's a time machine in *disguise*.'

Peter looked at the time machine. On the one hand he didn't believe Henry for one minute. This was just one of Henry's tricks. Peter was a hundred million billion percent certain Henry was lying.

On the other hand, what if Henry *was* telling the truth for once and there was a real time machine in his sitting room?

'If it *is* a time machine I want to have a go,' said Peter.

'You can't. You're too young,' said Henry.

'Am not.'

'Are too.'

Perfect Peter stuck out his bottom lip.

'I don't believe you anyway.'

Horrid Henry was outraged.

'Okay, I'll prove it. I'll go to the future right now. Stand back. Don't move.'

Horrid Henry leapt into the box and closed the lid. The time machine began to shudder and shake.

Then everything was still for a very long time.

Perfect Peter didn't know what to do. What if Henry was gone – for ever? What if he were stuck in the future?

I could have his room, thought Peter. I could watch whatever I wanted on telly. I could—

Suddenly the box tipped over and Horrid Henry staggered out.

'Wh-wh- where am I?' he stuttered. Then he collapsed on the floor.

Peter stared at Henry.

Henry stared wildly at Peter.

'I've been to the future!' gasped Henry, panting. 'It was amazing. Wow. I met my great-great-great-grandson. He still lives in this house. And he looks just like me.'

'So he's ugly,' muttered Peter.

'What – did – you – say?' hissed Henry.

'Nothing,' said Peter quickly. He didn't know what to think. 'Is this a trick, Henry?'

'Course it isn't,' said Henry. 'And just for that I won't let you have a go.'

'I can if I want to,' said Peter.

'You keep away from my time machine,' said Henry. 'One wrong move and you'll get blasted into the future.'

Perfect Peter walked a few steps towards the time machine. Then he paused.

'What's it like in the future?'

'Boys wear dresses,' said Horrid Henry. 'And lipstick. People talk Ugg language. *You'd* probably like it. Everyone just eats vegetables.'

'Really?'

'And kids have loads of homework.'

Perfect Peter loved homework.

'Ooohh.' This Peter *had* to see. Just in case Henry *was* telling the truth.

'I'm going to the future and you can't stop me,' said Peter.

'Go ahead,' said Henry. Then he snorted. 'You can't go looking like that!'

'Why not?' said Peter.

''Cause everyone will laugh at you.'

Perfect Peter hated people laughing at him.

'Why?'

'Because to them you'll look weird. Are you sure you really want to go to the future?'

'Yes,' said Peter.

'Are you sure you're sure?'

'YES,' said Peter.

'Then I'll get you ready,' said Henry solemnly.

'Thank you, Henry,' said Peter. Maybe he'd been wrong about Henry. Maybe going to the future had turned him into a nice brother.

Horrid Henry dashed out of the sitting room.

Perfect Peter felt a quiver of excitement. The future. What if Henry really was telling the truth?

Horrid Henry returned carrying a large wicker basket. He pulled out an old red dress of Mum's, some lipstick, and a black frothy drink.

'Here, put this on,' said Henry.

Perfect Peter put on the dress. It dragged onto the floor.

'Now, with a bit of lipstick,' said Horrid Henry,

applying big blobs of red lipstick all over Peter's face, 'you'll fit right in. Perfect,' he said, standing back to admire his handiwork. 'You look just like a boy from the future.'

'Okay,' said Perfect Peter.

'Now listen carefully,' said Henry. 'When you arrive, you won't be able to speak the language unless you drink this bibble babble drink. Take this with you and drink it when you get there.'

Henry held out the frothy black drink from his Dungeon Drink Kit. Peter took it.

'You can now enter the time machine.'

Peter obeyed. His heart was pounding.

'Don't get out until the time machine has stopped moving completely. Then count to twenty-five, and open the hatch very very slowly. You don't want a bit of you in the twenty-third century, and the rest here in the twenty-first. Good luck.'

Henry swirled the box round and round and round. Peter began to feel dizzy. The drink sloshed on the floor.

Then everything was still.

Peter's head was spinning. He counted to twenty-five, then crept out.

He was in the sitting room of a house that looked just like his. A boy wearing a bathrobe and silver waggly antennae with his face painted in blue stripes stood in front of him.

'Ugg?' said the strange boy.

'Henry?' said Peter.

'Uggg uggg bleuch ble bloop,' said the boy.

'Uggg uggg,' said Peter uncertainly.

'Uggh uggh drink ugggh,' said the boy, pointing to Peter's bibble babble drink.

Peter drank the few drops which were left.

'I'm Zog,' said Zog. 'Who are you?'

'I'm Peter,' said Peter.

'Ahhhhh! Welcome! You must be my great-great-great-uncle Peter. Your very nice brother Henry told me all about you when he visited me from the past.'

'Oh, what did he say?' said Peter.

'That you were an ugly toad.'

'I am not,' said Peter. 'Wait a minute,' he added suspiciously. 'Henry said that boys wore dresses in the future.'

'They do,' said Zog quickly. 'I'm a girl.'

'Oh,' said Peter. He gasped. Henry would *never* in a million years say he was a girl. Not even if he were being poked with red hot pokers. Could it be. . .

Peter looked around. 'This looks just like my sitting room.'

Zog snorted.

'Of course it does, Uncle Pete. This is now the Peter Museum. You're famous in the future. Everything has been kept exactly as it was.'

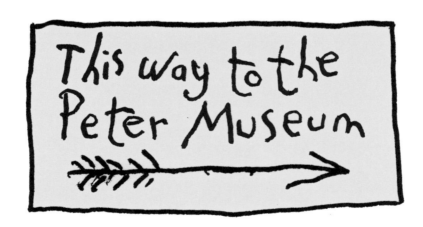

Peter beamed. He was famous in the future. He always knew he'd be famous. A Peter Museum! He couldn't wait to tell Spotless Sam and Tidy Ted.

There was just one more thing . . .

'What about Henry?' he asked. 'Is he famous too?'

'Nah,' said Zog smoothly. 'He's known as What's-His-Name, Peter's older brother.'

Ahh. Peter swelled with pride. Henry was in his lowly place, at last. That proved it. He'd really travelled to the future!

Peter looked out the window. Strange how the future didn't look so different from his own time.

Zog pointed.

'Our spaceships,' he announced.

Peter stared. Spaceships looked just like cars.

'Why aren't they flying?' said Peter.

'Only at night time,' said Zog. 'You can either drive 'em or fly 'em.'

'Wow,' said Peter.

'Don't *you* have spaceships?' said Zog.

'No,' said Peter. 'Cars.'

'I didn't know they had cars in olden days,' said Zog. 'Do you have blitzkatrons and zappersnappers?'

'No,' said Peter. 'What – '

The front door slammed. Mum walked in. She stared at Peter.

'What on earth. . .'

'Don't be scared,' said Peter. 'I'm Peter. I come from the past. I'm your great-great-great grandfather.'

Mum looked at Peter.

Peter looked at Mum.

'Why are you wearing my dress?' said Mum.

'It's not one of *yours*, silly,' said Peter. 'It belonged to my mum.'

'I see,' said Mum.

'Come on, Uncle Pete,' said Zog quickly, taking Peter firmly by the arm, 'I'll show you our supersonic hammock in the garden.'

'Okay, Zog,' said Peter happily.

Mum beamed.

'It's so lovely to see you playing nicely with your brother, Henry.'

Perfect Peter stood still.

'What did you call him?'

'Henry,' said Mum.

Peter felt a chill.

'So his name's not Zog? And he's not a girl?'

'Not the last time I looked,' said Mum.

'And this house isn't . . . the Peter Museum?'

Mum glared at Henry. 'Henry! Have you been teasing Peter again?'

'Ha ha tricked you!' shrieked Henry. 'Nah nah ne nah nah, wait till I tell everybody!'

'NO!' squealed Peter.

'NOOOOOOO!'

How *could* he have believed his horrible brother?

'Henry! You horrid boy! Go to your room! No TV for the rest of the day,' said Mum.

But Horrid Henry didn't care. The Mega–Mean Time Machine would go down in history as his greatest trick ever.

HOW TO BUILD YOUR OWN TIME MACHINE

1. Find huge box.
2. Load it with dials and gadgets.
3. Keep it away from grubby-fingered brothers and sisters.

Ugg Language Phrase Book

Uggg uggg bleuch ble bloop = Give me all your money

Uggga lugga = Wormy worm

Uggla mugla ugh? = Why are you so ugly?

Chgg ugggg = Chocolate

Ug mug ugguz lugga! = Out of my way, worm!

Ug mug ugguz tugga! = Out of my way, toad!

Uggla mugla ugh, lugga?

HORRID HENRY'S PERFECT DAY

Henry was horrid.

Everyone said so, even his mother.

Henry threw food, Henry snatched, Henry pushed and shoved and pinched. Even his teddy, Mr Kill, avoided him when possible.

His parents despaired.

'What are we going to do about that horrid boy?' sighed Mum.

'How did two people as nice as us have such a horrid child?' sighed Dad.

When Horrid Henry's parents took Henry to school they walked behind him and pretended he was not theirs.

Children pointed at Henry and whispered to their parents, 'That's Horrid Henry.'

'He's the boy who threw my jacket in the mud.'

'He's the boy who squashed Billy's beetle.'

'He's the boy who . . .'

Fill in whatever terrible deed you like.

Horrid Henry was sure to have done it.

Horrid Henry had a younger brother. His name was Perfect Peter.

Perfect Peter always said 'Please' and 'Thank you'. Perfect Peter loved vegetables.

Perfect Peter always used a hankie and never, ever picked his nose.

'Why can't you be perfect like Peter?' said Henry's Mum every day.

As usual, Henry pretended not to hear. He continued melting Peter's crayons on the radiator.

But Horrid Henry started to think.

'What if *I* were perfect?' thought Henry. 'I wonder what would happen.'

When Henry woke the next morning, he did not wake Peter by pouring water on Peter's head.

Peter did not scream.

This meant Henry's parents overslept and Henry and Peter were late for Cubs.

Henry was very happy.

Peter was very sad to be late for Cubs.

But because he was perfect, Peter did not whine or complain.

On the way to Cubs Henry did not squabble with Peter over who sat in front. He did not pinch Peter and he did not shove Peter.

Back home, when Perfect Peter built a castle, Henry did not knock it down. Instead, Henry sat on the sofa and read a book.

Mum and Dad ran into the room.

'It's awfully quiet in here,' said Mum. 'Are you being horrid, Henry?'

'No,' said Henry.

'Peter, is Henry knocking your castle down?'

Peter longed to say 'yes'. But that would be a lie.

'No,' said Peter.

He wondered why Henry was behaving so strangely.

'What are you doing, Henry?' said Dad.

'Reading a wonderful story about some super mice,' said Henry.

Dad had never seen Henry read a book before. He checked to see if a comic was hidden inside.

There was no comic. Henry was actually reading a book.

'Hmmmm,' said Dad.

It was almost time for dinner. Henry was hungry and went into the kitchen where Dad was cooking.

But instead of shouting, 'I'm starving! Where's my food?' Henry said, 'Dad, you look tired. Can I help get supper ready?'

'Don't be horrid, Henry,' said Dad, pouring peas into boiling water. Then he stopped.

'What did you say, Henry?' asked Dad.

'Can *I* help, Dad?' said Perfect Peter.

'I asked if you needed any help,' said Henry.

'I asked first,' said Peter.

'Henry will just make a mess,' said Dad. 'Peter, would you peel the carrots while I sit down for a moment?'

'Of course,' said Perfect Peter.

Peter washed his spotless hands.

Peter put on his spotless apron.

Peter rolled up his spotless sleeves.

Peter waited for Henry to snatch the peeler.

But Henry laid the table instead.

Mum came into the kitchen.

'Smells good,' she said. 'Thank you, darling Peter, for laying the table. What a good boy you are.'

Peter did not say anything.

'I laid the table, Mum,' said Henry.

Mum stared at him.

'You?' said Mum.

'Me,' said Henry.

'Why?' said Mum.

Henry smiled.

'To be helpful,' he said.

'You've done something horrid, haven't you, Henry?' said Dad.

'No,' said Henry. He tried to look sweet.

'I'll lay the table tomorrow,' said Perfect Peter.

'Thank you, angel,' said Mum.

'Dinner is ready,' said Dad.

The family sat down at the table.

Dinner was spaghetti and meatballs with peas and carrots.

Henry ate his dinner with his knife and fork and spoon.

He did not throw peas at Peter and he did not slurp.

He did not chew with his mouth open and he did not slouch.

'Sit properly, Henry,' said Dad.

'I am sitting properly,' said Henry.

Dad looked up from his plate. He looked surprised.

'So you are,' he said.

Perfect Peter could not eat. Why wasn't Henry throwing peas at him?

Peter's hand reached slowly for a pea.

When no one was looking, he flicked the pea at Henry.

'Ouch,' said Henry.

'Don't be horrid, Henry,' said Mum.

Henry reached for a fistful of peas. Then Henry remembered he was being perfect and stopped.

Peter smiled and waited. But no peas bopped him on the head.

Perfect Peter did not understand. Where was the foot that always kicked him under the table?

Slowly, Peter stretched out his foot and kicked Henry.

'OUCH,' said Henry.

'Don't be horrid, Henry,' said Dad.

'But I . . .' said Henry, then stopped.

Henry's foot wanted to kick Perfect Peter round the block. Then Henry remembered he was being perfect and continued to eat.

'You're very quiet tonight, Henry,' said Dad.

'The better to enjoy my lovely dinner,' said Henry.

'Henry, where are your peas and carrots?' asked Mum.

'I ate them,' said Henry. 'They were delicious.'

Mum looked on the floor. She looked under Henry's chair. She looked under his plate.

'You ate your peas and carrots?' said Mum slowly. She felt Henry's forehead.

'Are you feeling all right, Henry?'

'Yeah,' said Horrid Henry. 'I'm fine, thank you for asking,' he added quickly.

Mum and Dad looked at each other. What was going on?

Then they looked at Henry.

'Henry, come here and let me give you a big kiss,' said Mum. 'You are a wonderful boy. Would you like a piece of fudge cake?'

Peter interrupted.

'No cake for me, thank you,' said Peter. 'I would rather have more vegetables.'

Henry let himself be kissed. Oh my, it was hard work being perfect.

He smiled sweetly at Peter.

'I would love some cake, thank you,' said Henry.

Perfect Peter could stand it no longer. He picked up his plate and aimed at Henry.

Then Peter threw the spaghetti.

Henry ducked.

Splat!

Spaghetti landed on Mum's head. Tomato sauce trickled down her neck and down her new blue fuzzy jumper.

Peter!!!!'

yelled Mum and Dad.

'YOU HORRID BOY!' yelled Mum.

'GO TO YOUR ROOM!!' yelled Dad.

Perfect Peter burst into tears and ran to his room.

Mum wiped spaghetti off her face. She looked very funny.

Henry tried not to laugh. He squeezed his lips together tightly.

But it was no use. He could not stop a laugh escaping.

'It's not funny!' shouted Dad.

'Go to your room!' shouted Mum.

But Henry didn't care.

Who would have thought being perfect would be such fun?

HORRID HENRY'S PERFECT DAY DIARY

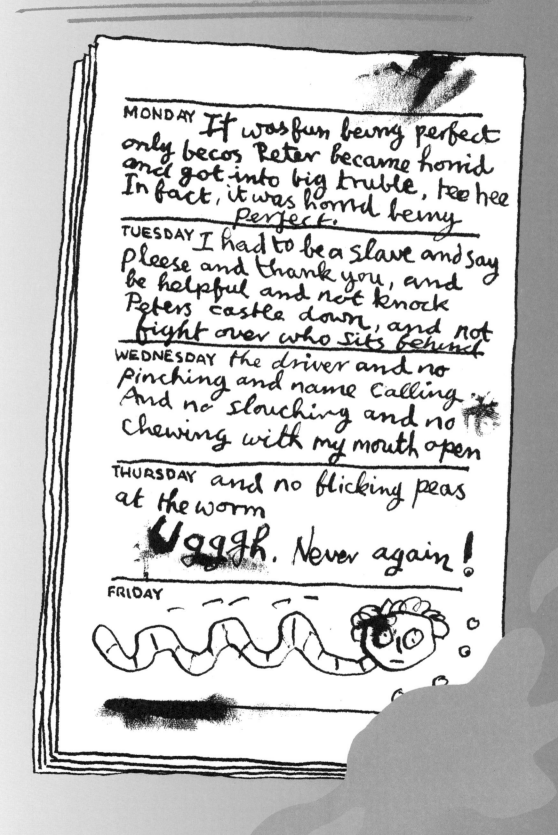

MONDAY It was fun being perfect only becos Peter became horrid and got into big truble, tee hee In fact, it was horrid being perfect.

TUESDAY I had to be a slave and say pleese and thank you, and be helpful and not knock Peters castle down, and not fight over who sits behind

WEDNESDAY the driver and no pinching and name calling. And no slouching and no chewing with my mouth open

THURSDAY and no flicking peas at the worm Ugggh. Never again!

FRIDAY

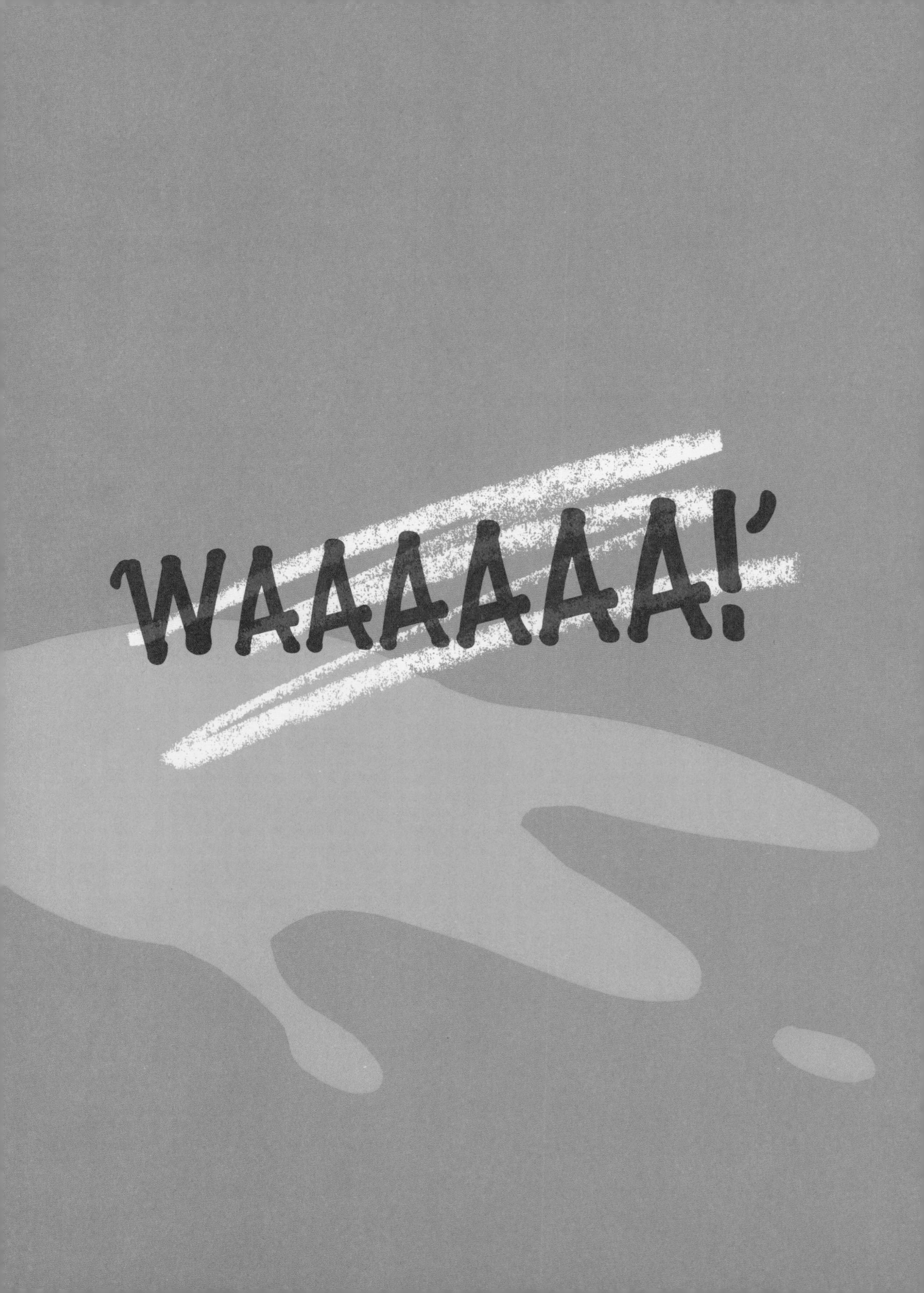
WAAAAAA!’

PERFECT PETER'S HORRiD DAY

'Henry, use your fork!' said Dad.

'*I'm* using my fork,' said Peter.

'Henry, sit down!' said Mum.

'*I'm* sitting down,' said Peter.

'Henry, stop spitting!' said Dad.

'*I'm* not spitting!' said Peter.

'Henry, chew with your mouth shut!' said Mum.

'*I'm* chewing with my mouth shut!' said Peter.

'Henry, don't make a mess!' said Dad.

'*I'm* not making a mess,' said Peter.

'What?' said Mum.

Perfect Peter was not having a perfect day.

Mum and Dad are too busy yelling at Henry all the time to notice how good *I* am, thought Peter.

When was the last time Mum and Dad had said, 'Marvellous, Peter, you're using your fork!'

'WONDERFUL, Peter, you're sitting down!'

'SUPERB, Peter, you're not spitting!'

'FABULOUS, Peter, you're chewing with your mouth shut!'

'PERFECT, Peter, you never make a mess!'

Perfect Peter dragged himself upstairs.

Everyone just expects me to be perfect, thought Peter, as he wrote his Aunt Ruby a thank you note for the super thermal vests. It's not fair.

From downstairs came the sound of raised voices.

'Henry, get your muddy shoes off the sofa!' yelled Dad.

'Henry, stop being so horrid!' yelled Mum.

Then Perfect Peter started to think.

What if *I* were horrid? thought Peter.

Peter's mouth dropped open. What a horrid thought! He looked around quickly, to see if anyone had noticed.

He was alone in his immaculate bedroom. No one would ever know he'd thought such a terrible thing.

But imagine being horrid. No, that would never do.

Peter finished his letter, read a few pages of his favourite magazine, *Best Boy*, got into bed and turned off his light without being asked.

Imagine being horrid.

What *if* I were horrid, thought Peter. I wonder what would happen?

When Peter woke up the next morning, he did not dash downstairs to get breakfast ready. Instead, he lazed in bed for an extra five minutes.

When he finally got out of bed Peter did not straighten the duvet.

Nor did Peter plump his pillows.

Instead Peter looked at his tidy bedroom and had a very wicked thought.

Quickly, before he could change his mind, he took off his pyjama top and did not fold it neatly. Instead he dropped it on the floor.

Mum came in.

'Good morning, darling. You must be tired, sleeping in.'

Peter hoped Mum would notice his untidy room.

But Mum did not say anything.

'Notice anything, Mum?' said Peter.

Mum looked around.

'No,' said Mum.

'Oh,' said Peter.

'What?' said Mum.

'I haven't made my bed,' said Peter.

'Clever you to remember it's washday,' said Mum. She stripped the sheets and duvet cover, then swooped and picked up Peter's pyjama top.

'Thank you, dear,' said Mum. She smiled and left.

Peter frowned. Clearly, he would need to work harder at being horrid.

He looked at his beautifully arranged books.

'No!' he gasped, as a dreadful thought sneaked into his head.

Then Peter squared his shoulders. Today was his horrid day, and horrid he would be. He went up to his books and knocked them over.

'HENRY!' bellowed Dad. 'Get up this minute!'

Henry slumped past Peter's door.

Peter decided he would call Henry a horrid name.

'Hello, Ugly,' said Peter. Then he went wild and stuck out his tongue.

Henry marched into Peter's bedroom. He glared at Peter.

'What did you call me?' said Henry.

Peter screamed.

Mum ran into the room.

'Stop being horrid, Henry! Look what a mess you've made in here!'

'He called me Ugly,' said Henry.

'Of course he didn't,' said Mum.

'He did too,' said Henry.

'Peter never calls people names,' said Mum. 'Now pick up those books you knocked over.'

'I didn't knock them over,' said Henry.

'Well, who did, then, the man in the moon?' said Mum.

Henry pointed at Peter.

'He did,' said Henry.

'*Did* you, Peter?' asked Mum.

Peter wanted to be really really horrid and tell a lie. But he couldn't.

'I did it, Mum,' said Peter. Boy, would he get told off now.

'Don't be silly, of course you didn't,' said Mum. 'You're just saying that to protect Henry.'

Mum smiled at Peter and frowned at Henry.

'Now leave Peter alone and get dressed,' said Mum.

'But it's the weekend,' said Henry.

'So?' said Mum.

'But Peter's not dressed.'

'I'm sure he was just about to get dressed before you barged in,' said Mum. 'See? He's already taken his pyjama top off.'

'I don't want to get dressed,' said Peter boldly.

'You poor boy,' said Mum. 'You must be feeling ill. Pop back into bed and I'll bring your breakfast up. Just let me put some clean sheets on.'

Perfect Peter scowled a tiny scowl. Clearly, he wasn't very good at being horrid yet. He would have to try harder.

At lunch Peter ate pasta with his fingers. No one noticed.

Then Henry scooped up pasta with both fists and slurped some into his mouth.

'Henry! Use your fork!' said Dad. Peter spat into his plate.

'Peter, are you choking?' said Dad.

Henry spat across the table.

'Henry! Stop that disgusting spitting this instant!' said Mum.

Peter chewed with his mouth open.

'Peter, is there something wrong with your teeth?' asked Mum.

Henry chomped and dribbled and gulped with his mouth as wide open as possible.

'Henry! This is your last warning. Keep your mouth shut when you eat!' shouted Dad.

Peter did not understand. Why didn't anyone notice how horrid he was? He stretched out his foot and kicked Henry under the table.

Henry kicked him back harder.

Peter shrieked.

Henry got told off. Peter got dessert.

Perfect Peter did not know what to do. No matter how hard he tried to be horrid, nothing seemed to work.

'Now boys,' said Mum, 'Grandma is coming for tea this afternoon. Please keep the house tidy and leave the chocolates alone.'

'What chocolates?' said Henry.

'Never you mind,' said Mum. 'You'll have some when Grandma gets here.'

Then Peter had a truly stupendously horrid idea. He left the table without waiting to be excused and sneaked into the sitting room.

Peter searched high. Peter searched low. Then Peter found a large box of chocolates hidden behind some books.

Peter opened the box. Then he took a tiny bite out of every single chocolate. When he found good ones with gooey chocolate fudge centres he ate them. The yucky raspberry and strawberry and lemon creams he put back.

Hee hee, thought Peter. He felt excited. What he had done was absolutely awful. Mum and Dad were sure to notice.

Then Peter looked round the tidy sitting room. Why not mess it up a bit?

Peter grabbed a cushion from the sofa. He was just about to fling it on the floor when he heard someone sneaking into the room.

'What are you doing?' said Henry.

'Nothing, Ugly,' said Peter.

'Don't call me Ugly, Toad,' said Henry.

'Don't call me Toad, Ugly,' said Peter.

'Toad!'

'Ugly!'

'TOAD!'

'UGLY!'

Mum and Dad ran in.

'Henry!' shouted Dad. 'Stop being horrid!'

'I'm not being horrid!' said Henry. 'Peter's calling me names.'

Mum and Dad looked at each other. What was going on?

'Don't lie, Henry,' said Mum.

'I did call him a name, Mum,' said Peter. 'I called him Ugly because he is ugly. So there.'

Mum stared at Peter.

Dad stared at Peter.

Henry stared at Peter.

'If Peter did call you a name, it's because you called him one first,' said Mum. 'Now leave Peter alone.'

Mum and Dad left.

'Serves you right, Henry,' said Peter.

'You're very strange today,' said Henry.

'No I'm not,' said Peter.

'Oh yes you are,' said Henry. 'You can't fool me. Listen, want to play a trick on Grandma?'

'No!' said Peter.

Ding dong.

'Grandma's here!' called Dad.

Mum, Dad, Henry, Peter and Grandma sat down
together in the sitting room.

'Let me take your bag, Grandma,' said Henry sweetly.

'Thank you dear,' said
Grandma.

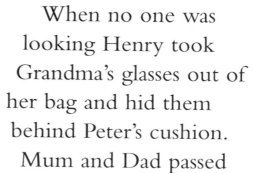

When no one was
looking Henry took
Grandma's glasses out of
her bag and hid them
behind Peter's cushion.

Mum and Dad passed
around tea and home-made
biscuits on the best china plates.

Peter sat on the edge of the sofa and held his breath.

Any second now Mum would get out the box of half–eaten chocolates.

Mum stood up and got the box.

'Peter, would you like to pass round the chocolates?' said Mum.

'Okay,' said Peter. His knees felt wobbly. Everyone was about to find out what a horrid thing he had done.

Peter held out the box.

'Would you like a chocolate, Mum?' said Peter. His heart pounded.

'No thanks,' said Mum.

'What about me?' said Henry.

'Would you like a chocolate, Dad?' said Peter. His hands shook.

'No thanks,' said Dad.

'What about me!' said Henry.

'Shh, Henry,' said Mum. 'Don't be so rude.'

'Would you like a chocolate, Grandma?' said Peter.

There was no escape now. Grandma loved chocolates.

'Yes, please!' said Grandma. She peered closely into the box. 'Let me see, what shall I choose? Now, where are my specs?'

Grandma reached into her bag and fumbled about.

'That's funny,' said Grandma. 'I was sure I'd brought them. Never mind.'

Grandma reached into the box, chose a chocolate and popped it into her mouth.

'Oh,' said Grandma. 'Strawberry cream. Go on, Peter, have a chocolate.'

'No thanks,' said Peter.

'WHAT ABOUT ME!' screamed Horrid Henry.

'None for you,' said Dad. 'That's not how you ask.'

Peter gritted his teeth. If no one was going to notice the chewed chocolates he'd have to do it himself.

'I will have a chocolate,' announced Peter loudly. 'Hey! Who's eaten all the fudge ones? And who's taken bites out of the rest?'

'Henry!' yelled Mum. 'I've told you a million times to leave the chocolates alone!'

'It wasn't me!' said Henry. 'It was Peter!'

'Stop blaming Peter,' said Dad.

'You know he never eats sweets.'

'It's not fair!' shrieked Henry. Then he snatched the box from Peter. 'I want some CHOCOLATES!'

Peter snatched it back. The open box fell to the floor. Chocolates flew everywhere.

'HENRY, GO TO YOUR ROOM!' yelled Mum.

'IT'S NOT FAIR!' screeched Henry. 'I'll get you for this Peter!'

Then Horrid Henry ran out of the room, slamming the door behind him.

Grandma patted the sofa beside her. Peter sat down. He could not believe it. What did a boy have to do to get noticed?

'How's my best boy?' asked Grandma.

Peter sighed.

Grandma gave him a big hug. 'You're the best boy in the world, Peter, did you know that?'

Peter glowed. Grandma was right! He was the best.

But wait. Today he was horrid.

NO! He was perfect. His horrid day was over.

He was much happier being perfect, anyway. Being horrid was horrible.

I've had my horrid day, thought Peter. Now I can be perfect again.

What a marvellous idea. Peter smiled and leaned back against the cushion.

CRUNCH!

'Oh dear,' said Grandma. 'That sounds like my specs. I wonder how they got there.'

Mum looked at Peter.

Dad looked at Peter.

'It wasn't me!' said Peter.

'Of course not,' said Grandma. 'I must have dropped them. Silly me.'

'Hmmmm,' said Dad.

Perfect Peter ran into the kitchen and looked about. Now that I'm perfect again, what good deeds can I do? he thought.

Then Peter noticed all the dirty tea cups and plates piled up on the worktop. He had never done the washing up all by himself before. Mum and Dad would be so pleased.

Peter carefully washed and dried all the dishes.

Then he stacked them up and carried them to the cupboard.

BOOOOOOO!

shrieked Horrid Henry, leaping out from behind the door.

Henry vanished.

Mum and Dad ran in.

The best china lay in pieces all over the floor.

Peter!!!!'

yelled Mum and Dad.

'YOU HORRID BOY!' yelled Mum.

'GO TO YOUR ROOM!' yelled Dad.

'But . . . But . . .' gasped Peter.

'NO BUTS!' shouted Mum. 'GO! Oh, my lovely dishes!'

Perfect Peter ran to his room.

'AHHHHHHHHHHHHH!'

shrieked Peter.

PERFECT PETER'S DIARY

It was boring being horrid.
I had to eat chocolate, mess up
my room, eat with my fingers,
chew with my mouth open,
and leave the table without
being excused.
I even tried to tell a lie.
Never again!

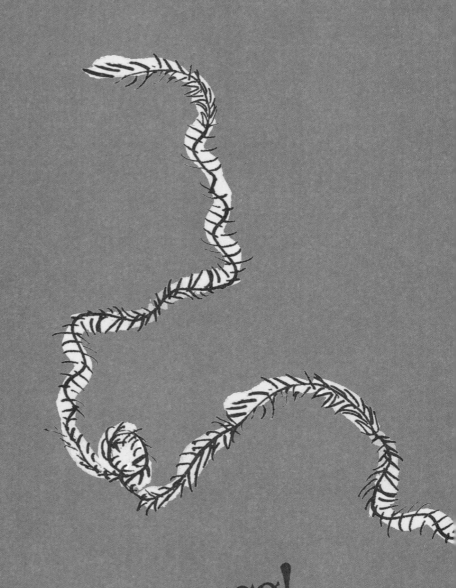

Uggg uggg chgg ugggg!
Ug mug ugguz uggga lugga tugga

HORRiD HENRY'S CHRISTMAS PRESENTS

Horrid Henry sat by the Christmas tree and stuffed himself full of the special sweets he'd nicked from the special Christmas Day stash when Mum and Dad weren't looking. After his triumph in the school Christmas play, Horrid Henry was feeling delighted with himself and with the world.

Granny and Grandpa, his grown-up cousins Pimply Paul and Prissy Polly, and their baby Vomiting Vera were coming to spend Christmas. Whoopee, thought Horrid Henry, because they'd all have to bring *him* presents. Thankfully, Rich Aunt Ruby and Stuck-Up Steve weren't coming. They were off skiing. Henry hadn't forgotten the dreadful lime green cardigan Aunt Ruby had given him last year. And much as he hated cousin Polly, anyone was better than Stuck-Up Steve, even someone who squealed all the time and had a baby who threw up on everyone.

Mum dashed into the sitting room, wearing a flour-covered apron and looking frantic. Henry choked down his mouthful of sweets.

'Right, who wants to decorate the tree?' said Mum. She held out a cardboard box brimming with tinsel and gold and silver and blue baubles.

'Me!' said Henry.

'Me!' said Peter.

Horrid Henry dashed to the box and scooped up as many shiny ornaments as he could.

'I want to put on the gold baubles,' said Henry.

'I want to put on the tinsel,' said Peter.

'Keep away from my side of the tree,' hissed Henry.

'You don't have a side,' said Peter.

'Do too.'

'Do not,' said Peter.

'I want to put on the tinsel *and* the baubles,' said Henry.

'But I want to do the tinsel,' said Peter.

'Tough,' said Henry, draping Peter in tinsel.

'Muuum!' wailed Peter. 'Henry's hogging all the decorations! And he's putting tinsel on me.'

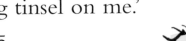

'Don't be horrid, Henry,' said Mum. 'Share with your brother.'

Peter carefully wrapped blue tinsel round the lower branches.

'Don't put it there,' said Henry, yanking it off. Trust Peter to ruin his beautiful plan.

'MUUUM!' wailed Peter.

'He's wrecking my design,' screeched Henry. 'He doesn't know how to decorate a tree.'

'But I wanted it there!' protested Peter. 'Leave my tinsel alone.'

'You leave my stuff alone then,' said Henry.

'He's wrecked my design!' shrieked Henry and Peter.

'Stop fighting, both of you!' shrieked Mum.

'He started it!' screamed Henry.

'Did not!'

'Did too!'

'That's enough,' said Mum. 'Now, whose turn is it to put the fairy on top?'

'I don't want to have that stupid fairy,' wailed Horrid Henry. 'I want to have Terminator Gladiator instead.'

'No,' said Peter. 'I want the fairy. We've always had the fairy.'

'Terminator!'

'Fairy!'

'TERMINATOR!'

'FAIRY!'

Slap Slap

'WAAAAAAA!'

'We're having the fairy,' said Mum firmly, 'and *I'll* put it on the tree.'

'NOOOOOO!'

screamed Henry. 'Why can't we do what I want to do? I never get to have what I want.'

'Liar!' whimpered Peter.

'I've had enough of this,' said Mum. 'Now get your presents and put them under the tree.'

Peter ran off.

Henry stood still.

'Henry,' said Mum. 'Have you finished wrapping your Christmas presents?'

Yikes, thought Horrid Henry. What am I going to

do now? The moment he'd been dreading for weeks had arrived.

'Henry! I'm not going to ask you again,' said Mum. 'Have you finished wrapping all your Christmas presents?'

'Yes!' bellowed Horrid Henry.

This was not entirely true. Henry had not finished wrapping his Christmas presents. In fact, he hadn't even started. The truth was, Henry had finished wrapping because he had no presents to wrap.

This was certainly *not* his fault. He *had* bought a few gifts, certainly. He knew Peter would love the box of green Day-Glo slime. And if he didn't, well, he knew who to give it to. And Granny and Grandpa and Mum and Dad and Paul and Polly would have adored the big boxes of chocolates Henry had won at the school fair. Could he help it if the chocolates had called his name so loudly that he'd been forced to eat them all? And

then Granny had been complaining about gaining weight. Surely it would have been very unkind to give her chocolate. And eating chocolate would have just made Pimply Paul's pimples worse. Henry'd done him a big favour eating that box.

And it was hardly Henry's fault when he'd needed extra goo for a raid on the Secret Club and Peter's present was the only stuff to hand. He'd *meant* to buy replacements. But he had so many things he needed to buy for himself that when he opened his skeleton bank to get out some cash for Christmas shopping, only 35p had rolled out.

'I've bought and wrapped all *my* presents, Mum,' said Perfect Peter. 'I've been saving my pocket money for months.'

'Whoopee for you,' said Henry.

'Henry, it's always better to give than to receive,' said Peter.

Mum beamed. 'Quite right, Peter.'

'Says who?' growled Horrid Henry. 'I'd much rather *get* presents.'

'Don't be so horrid, Henry,' said Mum.

'Don't be so selfish, Henry,' said Dad.

Horrid Henry stuck out his tongue. Mum and Dad gasped.

'You horrid boy,' said Mum.

'I just hope Father Christmas didn't see that,' said Dad.

'Henry,' said Peter, 'Father Christmas won't bring you any presents if you're bad.'

'AAARRRGGHHH!'

Horrid Henry sprang at Peter. He was a grizzly bear guzzling a juicy morsel.

'AAAAIIEEE,' wailed Peter. 'Henry pinched me.'

'Henry! Go to your room,' said Mum.

'Fine!' screamed Horrid Henry, stomping off and slamming the door. Why did he get stuck with the world's meanest and most horrible parents? *They* certainly didn't deserve any presents.

Presents! Why couldn't he just *get* them? Why oh why did he have to *give* them? Giving other people presents was such a waste of his hard-earned money. Every time he gave a present it meant something he couldn't buy for himself. Goodbye chocolate. Goodbye comics. Goodbye Deluxe Goo-Shooter. And then, if you bought anything good, it was so horrible having to give it away. He'd practically cried having to give Ralph that Terminator Gladiator poster for his birthday. And the Mutant Max lunchbox Mum made him give Kasim still made him gnash his teeth whenever he saw Kasim with it.

Now he was stuck, on Christmas Eve, with no money, and no presents to give anyone, deserving or not.

And then Henry had a wonderful, spectacular idea. It was so wonderful, and so spectacular, that he couldn't believe he hadn't thought of it before. Who said he had to *buy* presents? Didn't Mum and Dad always say it was the *thought* that counted? And oh boy was he thinking.

Granny was sure to love a Mutant Max comic. After all, who wouldn't? Then when she'd finished enjoying it, he could borrow it back. Horrid Henry rummaged under his bed and found a recent copy. In fact, it would be a shame if Grandpa got jealous of Granny's great present. Safer to give them each one, thought Henry, digging deep into his pile to find one with the fewest torn pages.

Now let's see, Mum and Dad. He could draw them a lovely picture. Nah, that would take too long. Even better, he could write them a poem.

Henry sat down at his desk, grabbed a pencil, and wrote:

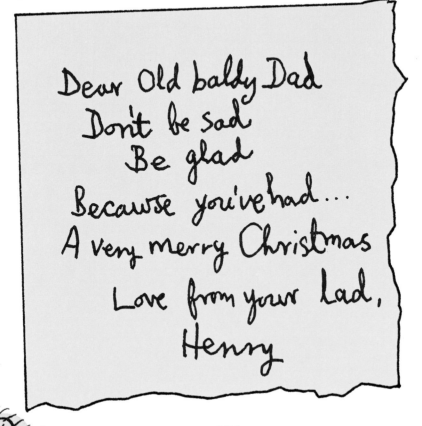

Dear Old baldy Dad
Don't be sad
Be glad
Because you've had...
A very merry Christmas
Love from your lad,
Henry

Not bad, thought Henry. Not bad. And so cheap!
Now one for Mum.

Dear Old wrinkly Mum
Don't be glum
Cause you've got a fat tum
And an even bigger bum
Ho ho ho hum
Love from your son,

Henry

Wow! It was hard finding so many words to rhyme
with *Mum* but he'd done it. And the poem was nice
and Christmassy with the 'ho ho ho'. *Son* didn't rhyme
but hopefully Mum wouldn't notice because she'd be
so thrilled with the rest of the poem. When he was
famous she'd be proud to show off the poem her son
had written specially for her.

Now, Polly. Hmmmn. She was always squeaking and
squealing about dirt and dust. Maybe a lovely kitchen
sponge? Or a rag she could use to mop up after Vera?

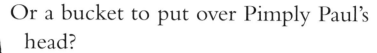

Or a bucket to put over Pimply Paul's head?

Wait. What about some soap?

Horrid Henry nipped into the bathroom. Yes! There was a tempting bar of blue soap going to waste in the soap dish by the bathtub. True, it had been used once or twice, but a bit of smoothing with his fingers would sort that out. In fact, Polly and Paul could share this present, it was such a good one.

Whistling, Horrid Henry wrapped up the soap in sparkling reindeer paper. He was a genius. Why hadn't he ever done this before? And a lovely rag from under the sink would be perfect as a gag for Vera.

That just left Peter and all his present problems would be over. A piece of chewing gum, only one careful owner? A collage of sweet wrappers which spelled out *Worm*? The unused comb Peter had given *him* last Christmas?

184

Aha. Peter loved bunnies. What better present than a picture of a bunny?

It was the work of a few moments for Henry to draw a bunny and slash a few blue lines across it to colour it in. Then he signed his name in big letters at the bottom. Maybe he should be a famous artist and not a poet when he grew up, he thought, admiring his handiwork. Henry had heard that artists got paid loads of cash just for stacking a few bricks or hurling paint at a white canvas. Being an artist sounded like a great job, since it left so much time for playing computer games.

Horrid Henry dumped his presents beneath the Christmas tree and sighed happily. This was one Christmas where he was sure to get a lot more than he gave.

Whoopee!

Who could ask for anything more?

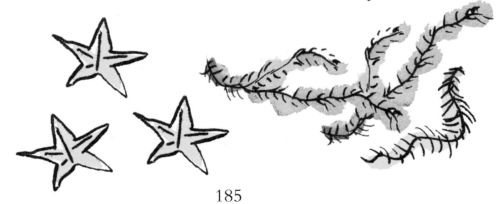

HORRID HENRY'S GIFT IDEAS

It's **NEVER** better to give than to receive. Spending hard-earned cash on presents for undeserving people is

My Bruv is THE beST Toad

Henry

my mum and Dad are The WORST Mum and the WORST DAD

Henry

Certificates

Henry.

Sweet wrapper collage

me by me

the worst part about Christmas.
Remember, it's the thought that
counts. And thoughts don't count.

Henry
Henry
Henry
Henry
Henry
Henry

My autograph

Drawings
of me

Miss Battleaxe
Henry

Rain
Henry

Peter
Henry

a black hole
Henry

a pet worm
Henry

Drawings

A plastic
bag (very
useful)

HORRiD HENRY'S FAMILY FACT FILE

(All the stuff they don't want anyone to know!!!)

Secret Dreams

Henry: to be a dictator and rule the world

*

Peter: to marry Miss Lovely

*

Mum: to be a tap dancer

Dad: to be a Rock'n'Roll god

*

Aunt Ruby: to be best friends with the Queen

*

Stuck-up Steve: to be a champion skier

*

Fluffy: to live in a house filled with mice

*

Fang: to be bigger than Fluffy

Deepest, Darkest Secrets

Mum: she sneaks sweets from the sweet jar

*

Dad: he is scared of injections

*

Peter: Miss Lovely once told him off for running in class

Stuck-up Steve: he can't sleep without Little Ducky

*

Henry: wouldn't you like to know!

Horrid Henry's Grisly Gallery

Blood Boil Bob

Lisping Lily

Santa

Mrs Mossy

Mr Mossy

Maggie

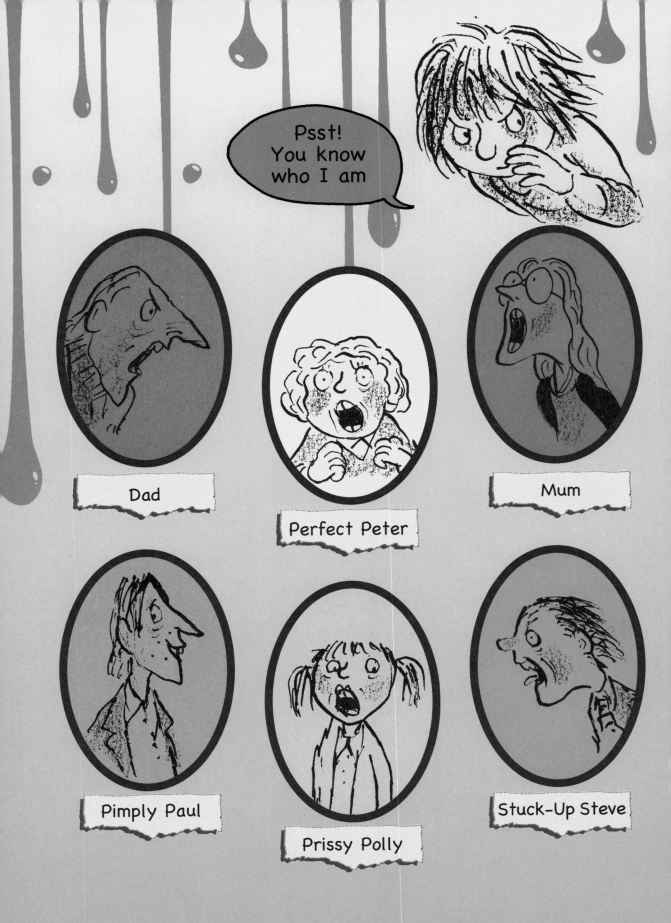

HORRID HENRY'S
Sleepover

Horrid Henry loved sleepovers. Midnight feasts! Pillow fights! Screaming and shouting! Rampaging till dawn!

The time he ate all the ice cream at Greedy Graham's and left the freezer door open! The time he jumped on all the beds at Dizzy Dave's and broke them all. And that time at Rude Ralph's when he — well, hmmn, perhaps better not mention that.

There was just one problem. No one would ever have Horrid Henry at their house for a sleepover more than once. Whenever Henry went to sleep at a friend's house, Mum and Dad were sure to get a call

at three a.m. from a demented
parent screaming at them to
pick up Henry immediately.

Horrid Henry couldn't
understand it. Parents were
so fussy. Even the parents of
great kids like Rude Ralph
and Greedy Graham. Who
cares about a little noise? Or
a broken bed? Big deal, thought
Horrid Henry.

It was no fun having friends sleep over at his
house. There was no rampaging and feasting at
Henry's. It was lights out as usual at nine o'clock,
no talking, no feasting, no fun.

So when New Nick, who had just joined Henry's
class, invited Henry to stay the night, Horrid Henry
couldn't believe his luck. New beds to bounce on.
New biscuit tins to raid. New places to rampage. Bliss!

Henry packed his sleepover bag as fast as he could.
Mum came in. She looked grumpy.

'Got your pyjamas?' she asked.

Henry never needed pyjamas at sleepovers
because he never went to bed.

'Got them,' said Henry. Just not
with him, he thought.

'Don't forget your toothbrush,' said Mum.

'I won't,' said Horrid Henry. He never forgot his toothbrush – he just chose not to bring it.

Dad came in. He looked even grumpier.

'Don't forget your comb,' said Dad.

Horrid Henry looked at his bulging backpack stuffed with toys and comics. Sadly, there was no room for a comb.

'I won't,' lied Henry.

'I'm warning you, Henry,' said Mum. 'I want you to be on best behaviour tonight.'

'Of course,' said Horrid Henry.

'I don't want any phone calls at three a.m. from Nick's parents,' said Dad. 'If I do, this will be your last sleepover ever. I mean it.'

NAG NAG NAG.

'All right,' said Horrid Henry.

Ding dong.

A woman opened the door. She was wearing a Viking helmet on her head and long flowing robes. Behind her stood a man in a velvet cloak holding back five enormous, snarling black dogs.

wOOF wOOF wOOF wOOF wOOF

'TRA LA LA BOOM-DY AY,' boomed a dreadful, earsplitting voice.

'Bravo, bravo!' shouted a chorus from the sitting room.

GRRRRRRR! growled the dogs.

Horrid Henry hesitated. Did he have the right house? Was New Nick an alien?

'Oh don't mind us, dear, it's our opera club's karaoke night,' trilled the Viking helmet.

'Nick!' bellowed the Cloak. 'Your friend is here.'

Nick appeared. Henry was glad to see he was not wearing a Viking helmet or a velvet cloak.

'Hi Henry,' said New Nick.

'Hi Nick,' said Horrid Henry.

A little girl toddled over, sucking her thumb.

'Henry, this is my sister, Lily,' said Nick.

Lily gazed at Horrid Henry.

'I love you, Henwy,' said Lisping Lily. 'Will you marry with me?'

'NO!' said Horrid Henry. Uggh. What a revolting thought.

'Go away, Lily,' said Nick.

Lily did not move.

'Come on, Nick, let's get out of here,' said Henry. No toddler was going to spoil his fun. Now, what would he do first, raid the kitchen, or bounce on the beds?

'Let's raid the kitchen,' said Henry.

'Great,' said Nick.

'Got any good sweets?' asked Henry.

'Loads!' said New Nick.

Yeah! thought Horrid Henry. His sleepover fun was beginning!

They sneaked into the kitchen. The floor was covered with dog blankets, overturned food bowls, clumps of dog hair, and gnawed dog bones. There were a few suspicious looking puddles. Henry hoped they were water.

'Here are the biscuits,' said Nick.

Henry looked. Were those dog hairs all over the jar?

'Uh, no thanks,' said Henry. 'How about some sweets?'

'Sure,' said Nick. 'Help yourself.'

He handed Henry a bar of chocolate. Yummy! Henry was about to take a big bite when he stopped. Were those – teeth marks in the corner?

'Raaa!' A big black shape jumped on Henry, knocked him down, and snatched the chocolate.

Nick's dad burst in.

'Rigoletto! Give that back!' said Nick's dad, yanking the chocolate out of the dog's mouth.

'Sorry about that, Henry,' he said, offering it back to Henry.

'Uhh, maybe later,' said Henry.

'Okay,' said Nick's dad, putting the slobbery chocolate back in the cupboard.

Eeew, gross, thought Horrid Henry.

'I love you, Henwy,' came a lisping voice behind him.

'AH HA HA HA HA HA HA HA!'

warbled a high, piercing voice from the sitting room.

Henry held his ears. Would the windows shatter?

'Encore!' shrieked the opera karaoke club.

'Will you marry with me?' asked Lisping Lily.

'Let's get out of here,' said Horrid Henry.

Horrid Henry leapt on Nick's bed.

Yippee, thought Horrid Henry. Time to get bouncing.

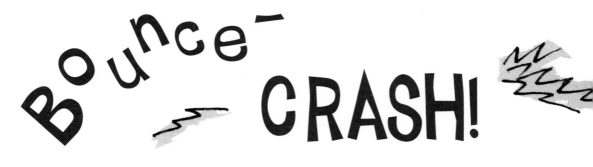

Bounce — CRASH!

The bed collapsed in a heap.

'What happened?' said Henry. 'I hardly did anything.'

'Oh, I broke the bed ages ago,' said Nick. 'Dad said he was tired of fixing it.'

Rats, thought Henry. What a lazy dad.

'How about a pillow fight?' said Henry.

'No pillows,' said Nick. 'The dogs chewed them.'

Hmmn.

They could sneak down and raid the freezer, but for some reason Henry didn't really want to go back into that kitchen.

'I know!' said Henry. 'Let's watch TV.'

'Sure,' said New Nick.

'Where is the TV?' said Henry.

'In the sitting room,' said Nick.

'But – the karaoke,' said Henry.

'Oh, they won't mind,' said Nick. 'They're used to noise in this house.'

'DUM DUM DE DUM DUMM DUM DE DUM DUMM DUM –'

Horrid Henry sat with his face pressed to the TV. He couldn't hear a word Mutant Max was shrieking with all that racket in the background.

'Maybe we should go to bed,' said Horrid Henry, sighing. Anything to get away from the noise.

'Okay,' said New Nick.

Phew, thought Horrid Henry. Peace at last.

SNORE! SNORE!

Horrid Henry turned over in his
sleeping bag and tried to get comfortable. He hated
sleeping on the floor. He hated sleeping with the
window open.

He hated sleeping with the radio on. And he hated
sleeping in the same room with someone who snored.

Awhooooooo! howled the winter wind through
the open window.

SNORE!
    SNORE!

'I'm just a lonesome cowboy, lookin' for a
lonesome cowgirl,' blared the radio.

WOOF WOOF WOOF barked the dogs.

'Yeowwwww!' squealed Henry, as five wet, smelly dogs pounced on him.

'Awhoooo!' howled the wind.

SNORE!

SNORE!

'TOREADOR – on guard!' boomed the opera karaoke downstairs.

Horrid Henry loved noise. But this was – too much.

He'd have to find somewhere else to sleep.

Horrid Henry flung open the bedroom door.

'I love you, Henwy,' said Lisping Lily.

Slam! Horrid Henry shut the bedroom door.

Horrid Henry did not move.

Horrid Henry did not breathe.

Then he opened the door a fraction.

'Will you marry with me, Henwy?'

Aaarrrgh!!!

Horrid Henry ran from the bedroom and barricaded himself in the linen cupboard. He settled down on a pile of towels.

Phew. Safe at last.

'I want to give you a big kiss, Henwy,' came a little voice beside him.

NOOOOOOOO!

It was three a.m.

'TRA LA LA

BOOM-DY AY!'

'— LONESOME COWBOY!'

SNORE!

SNORE!

AWHOOOOOOOOOOOOOO!

WOOF! WOOF! WOOF!

Horrid Henry crept to the hall phone and dialled his number.

Dad answered.

'I'm so sorry about Henry, do you want us to come and get him?' Dad mumbled.

'Yes,' wailed Horrid Henry. 'I need my rest!'

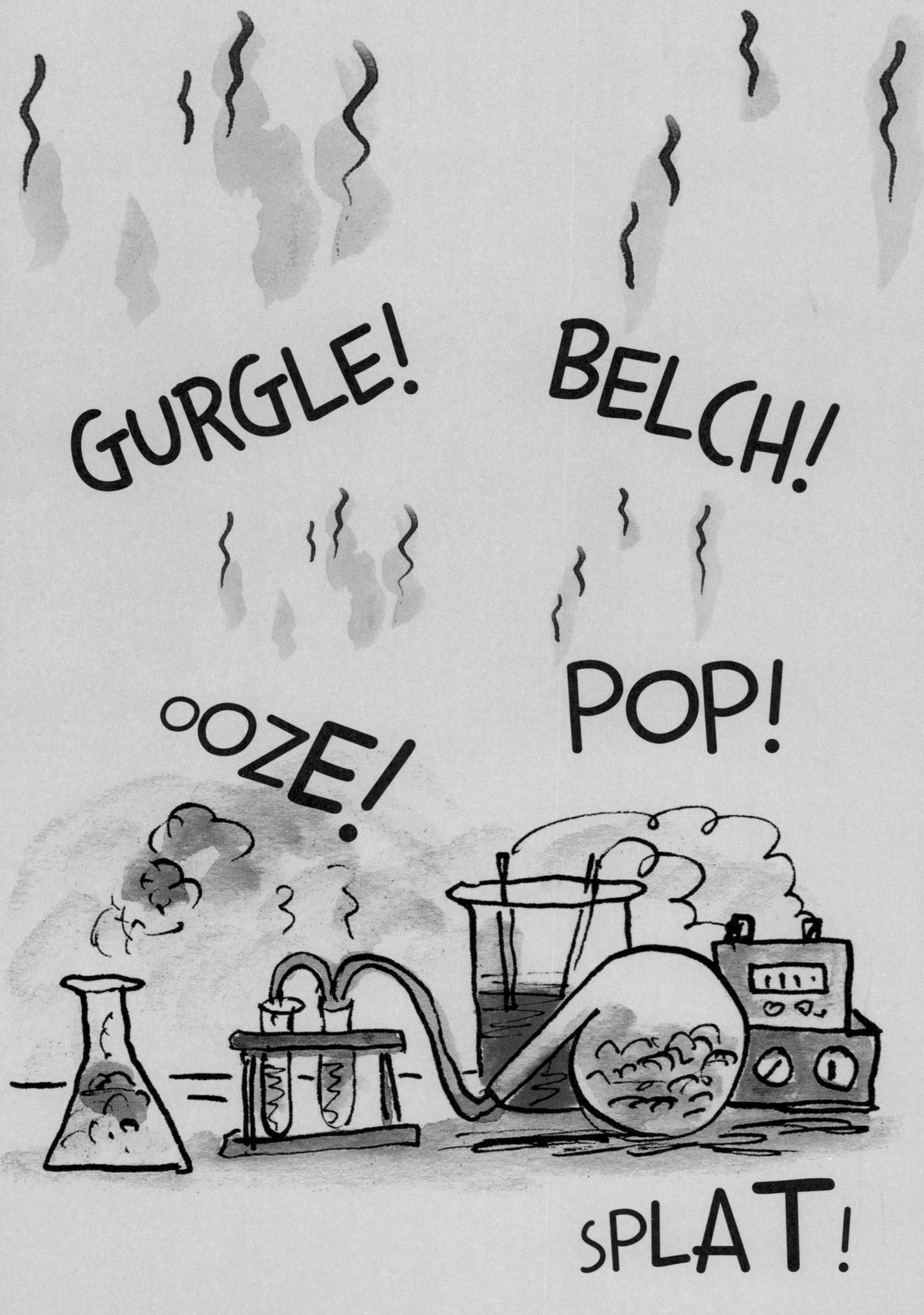
GURGLE!
BELCH!
OOZE!
POP!
SPLAT!

HORRID HENRY
and the Dinner Guests

FIZZ! POP! GURGLE! BANG!

Horrid Henry sat on the kitchen floor watching his new Dungeon Drink kit brew a bubbly purple potion.

BELCH! CRUNCH! OOZE! SPLAT!

Beside it, a Grisly Ghoul Grub box heaved and spewed some Rotten Crispies.

Dad dashed into the kitchen.

'Want a crisp?' said Henry, smirking.

'No!' said Dad, putting on his apron. 'And I've told you before to play with those disgusting kits in your bedroom.'

Why Henry's grandmother had bought him those terrible toys for Christmas he would never know.

'Henry, I want you to listen carefully,' said Dad, feverishly rolling out pastry. 'Mum's new boss and her husband are coming to dinner in an hour. I want total cooperation and perfect behaviour.'

'Yeah, yeah,' said Henry, his eyes glued to the frothing machine.

Horrid Henry's parents didn't have guests for dinner very often. The last time they did Henry had sneaked downstairs, eaten the entire chocolate cake Dad had baked for dessert and then been sick all over the sofa. The time before that he'd put whoopee cushions on all the guests' seats,

bitten Peter, and broken the banister by sliding down it.

Dad started getting pots and pans down.

'What are you cooking?' said Perfect Peter, tidying up his stamps.

'Salmon wrapped in pastry with lime and ginger,' said Dad, staring at his list.

'Yummy!' said Perfect Peter. 'My favourite!'

'Yuck!' said Horrid Henry. 'I want pizza. What's for pudding?'

'Chocolate mousse,' said Dad.

'Can I help?' said Peter.

'Of course,' said Mum, smiling. 'You can pass round the nuts and crisps when Mr and Mrs Mossy arrive.'

Nuts? Crisps? Henry's ears perked up.

'I'll help too,' said Henry.

Mum looked at him. 'We'll see,' she said.

'I don't think Henry should pass round the nuts,' said Peter. 'He'll only eat them himself.'

'Shut up, Peter,' snarled Henry.

'Mum! Henry told me to shut up!' wailed Peter.

'Henry! Stop being horrid,' muttered Dad, grating ginger and squeezing limes.

While Dad rolled up salmon in pastry, Mum dashed about setting the table with the best china.

'Hey! You haven't set enough places,' said Henry. 'You've only set the table for four.'

'That's right,' said Mum. 'Mrs Mossy, Mr Mossy, Dad and me.'

'What about me?' said Henry.

'And me?' said Peter.

'This is a grown-ups' party,' said Mum.

'You want me . . . to go . . . to bed?' Henry stuttered. 'I'm not . . . eating with you?'

'No,' said Dad.

'It's not fair!' shrieked Henry. 'What am I having for supper then?'

'A cheese sandwich,' said Dad. 'We've got to get ready for the guests. I'm already two minutes behind my schedule.'

'I'm not eating this swill!' shrieked Henry, shoving the sandwich off his plate. 'I want pizza!'

'That's all right, Dad,' said Peter, tucking into his sandwich. 'I understand that grown-ups need to be by themselves sometimes.'

Henry lunged at Peter. He was a cannibal trussing his victim for the pot.

'AAARGHH!' shrieked Peter.

'That's it, Henry, go to bed!' shouted Mum.

'I won't!' screamed Henry. 'I want chocolate mousse!'

'Go upstairs and stay upstairs!' shouted Mum.

Ding dong!

'Aaagh!' squealed Dad. 'They're early! I haven't finished the mousse yet.'

Horrid Henry stomped upstairs to his bedroom and slammed the door.

He was so angry he could hardly speak. The injustice of it all. Why should he go to bed while Mum and Dad were downstairs having fun and eating

chocolate mousse? The delicious smell of melting chocolate wafted into his nostrils. Henry's tummy rumbled. If Mum and Dad thought he'd stay in bed while they all had fun downstairs they had rocks for brains.

SCREEEECH! SCREEEECH!

Perfect Peter must be playing his cello for Mum and Dad and the guests. Which meant . . . Horrid Henry smiled. The coast was clear. Hello, nuts, here I come, thought Henry.

Henry tiptoed downstairs. The screechy-scratchy sounds continued from the sitting room.

Horrid Henry sneaked into the empty kitchen. There were the bowls of nuts and crisps and the drinks all ready to serve.

Cashews, my favourite. I'll just have a few, he thought.

Chomp. Chomp. Chomp.

Hmmn, boy, those nuts were good. Irresistible, really, thought Henry. A few more would go down a treat. And, if he poured the remaining nuts into a smaller bowl, no one would notice how many he'd eaten.

CHOMP! CHOMP! CHOMP!

Just one more, thought Henry, and that's it.

Horrid Henry swizzled his fingers round the nut bowl.

Uh-oh. There were only three nuts left.

Yikes, thought Henry. Now I'm in trouble.

FIZZ! POP! GURGLE! BANG! BELCH! CRUNCH! OOZE! SPLAT!

Horrid Henry looked at his Grisly Grub box and Dungeon Drink kit and bopped himself on the head. What an idiot he was. What better time to try out his grisly grub than . . . now?

Henry examined the Rotten Crispies he'd made earlier. They looked like crisps, but certainly didn't taste like them. The only problem was, what to do with the good crisps?

219

Yum yum! thought Henry, crunching crisps as fast as he could. Then he refilled the bowl with Rotten Crispies.

Next, Henry poured two frothing dungeon drinks into glasses, and put them on the tray.

Perfect, thought Henry. Now to make some Nasty Nuts to replace all those cashews.

The kitchen door opened. Dad came in.

'What are you doing, Henry? I told you to go to bed.'

'Mum said I could serve the nuts,' said Henry, lying shamelessly. Then he grabbed the two bowls and escaped.

The sound of applause came from the sitting room. Perfect Peter bowed modestly.

'Isn't he adorable?' said Mrs Mossy.

'And so talented,' said Mr Mossy.

'Hello, Mr and Mrs Bossy,' said Henry.

Mum looked horrified.

'Mossy, not Bossy, dear,' said Mum.

'But that's what you call them, Mum,' said Henry, smiling sweetly.

'Henry is just going to bed,' said Mum, blushing.

'No I wasn't,' said Henry. 'I was going to serve the nuts and crisps. Don't you remember?'

'Oooh, I love nuts,' said Mrs Mossy.

'I told you to stay upstairs,' hissed Mum.

'Muuuum,' wailed Peter. 'You said I could serve the guests.'

'You can serve the crisps, Peter,' said Henry graciously, handing him the bowl of Rotten Crispies. 'Would you like a cashew, Mrs Bossy?'

'Mossy!' hissed Mum.

'Ooh, cashews, my favourite,' said Mrs Mossy. She plunged her fingers into the mostly empty nut bowl, and finally scooped up the remaining three.

Henry snatched two back.

'You're only supposed to have one nut at a time,' he said. 'Don't be greedy.'

'Henry!' said Mum. 'Don't be rude.'

'Want a nut?' said Henry, waving the bowl in front of Mr Mossy.

'Why, yes, I . . .' said Mr Mossy. But he was too late. Henry had already moved away to serve Mum.

'Want a nut?' he asked.

Mum's hand reached out to take one, but Henry quickly whisked the bowl away.

'Henry!' said Mum.

'Do have some crisps, Mrs Mossy,' said Perfect Peter. Mrs Mossy scooped up a large handful of

Rotten Crispies and then stuffed them in her mouth.

Her face went purple, then pink, then green.

'BLECCCCCH!' she spluttered, spitting them out all over Mr Mossy.

'Peter, run and get Mrs Mossy something to drink!' shouted Mum.

Peter dashed to the kitchen and brought back a frothing drink.

'Thank you,' gasped Mrs Mossy, taking the glass and gulping it down.

'YUCK!' she spluttered, spitting it out. 'Are you trying to poison me, you horrible child?' she choked, flailing her arms and crashing into Dad, who had just walked in carrying the drinks tray.

CRASH! SPLASH!

Mum, Dad, Peter, and Mr and Mrs Mossy were soaked.

'Peter, what have you done?' shouted Mum.

Perfect Peter burst into tears and ran out of the room.

'Oh dear, I'm so sorry,' said Mum.

'Never mind,' said Mrs Mossy, through gritted teeth.

'Sit down, everyone,' said Henry. 'I'm going to do a show now.'

'No,' said Mum.

'No,' said Dad.

'But Peter did one,' howled Henry. 'I WANT TO DO A SHOW!'

'All right,' said Mum. 'But just a quick one.'

Henry sang. The guests held their ears.

'Not so loud, Henry,' said Mum.

Henry pirouetted, trampling on the guests.

'Ooof,' said Mr Mossy, clutching his toe.

'Aren't you finished, Henry?' said Dad.

Henry juggled, dropping both balls on Mrs Mossy's head.

'Ow,' said Mrs Mossy.

'Now I'll show you my new karate moves,' said Henry.

'NO!' shouted Mum and Dad.

But before anyone could stop him Henry's arms and legs flew out in a mad karate dance.

'HI-YA!' shrieked Henry, knocking into Mr Mossy.

Mr Mossy went flying across the room.

Whoosh! Off flew his toupee.

Click-clack! Out bounced his false teeth.

'Reginald!' gasped Mrs Mossy. 'Are you all right? Speak to me!'

'Uggghhh,' groaned Mr Mossy.

'Isn't that great?' said Henry. 'Who wants to go next?'

'What's that terrible smell?' choked Mrs Mossy.

'Oh no!' screamed Dad. 'The salmon is burning!'

Mum and Dad ran into the kitchen, followed by Mr and Mrs Mossy.

Smoke poured from the oven. Mum grabbed a tea towel and started whacking the burning salmon.

WHACK! THWACK!

'Watch out!' screamed Dad.

The towel thwacked the bowl of chocolate mousse and sent it crashing to the ground.

 **SPLAT!**

There was chocolate mousse on the floor. There was chocolate mousse on the ceiling. And there was chocolate mousse all over Mr and Mrs Mossy, Mum, Dad and Henry.

'Oh no,' said Mum, holding her head in her hands. Then she burst into tears. 'What are we going to do?'

'Leave it to me, Mum,' said Horrid Henry. He marched to the phone.

'Pizza Delight?' he said. 'I'd like to order a mega-whopper, please.'

Poor Mr Mossy has lost his toupee. What style should he wear next?

POP! GURGLE! FIZZ!

BANG! CRUNCH! OOZE! BELCH! SPLAT!

Dungeon Drink Recipe
Beetroot juice
Mushroom Soup
Cola
Bits of liquorice
Lots of Tabasco Sauce
Chilli powder

The
GOO-SHOOTER
CHAMPION!

The BEST!

UNBEATABLE!

A STAR!

FABULOUS!

The
ICE-CREAM
EATING KING!

HENRY
A STAR IS BORN

HORRiD HENRY
Minds his Manners

'Henry and Peter! You've got mail!' said Mum.

Henry and Peter thundered down the stairs. Horrid Henry snatched his letter and tore open the green envelope. The foul stink of mouldy socks wafted out.

Yo Henry!
Marvin the Maniac here. You sound just like the kind of crazy guy we want on GROSS-OUT! Be at TV Centre next Saturday at 9.00 a.m. and gross us out! It's a live broadcast, so anything can happen!

Marvin

'I've been invited to be a contestant on *Gross-Out!*' screamed Henry, dancing up and down the stairs. It was a dream come true. 'I'll be shooting it out with Tank Thomas and Tapioca Tina while eating as much ice cream as I can!'

'Absolutely not!' said Mum. 'You will not go on that disgusting show!'

'Agreed,' said Dad. 'That show is revolting.'

'It's meant to be revolting!' said Horrid Henry. 'That's the point.'

'N–O spells no,' said Mum.

'You're the meanest, most horrible parents in the whole world,' screamed Henry. 'I hate you!' He threw himself on the sofa and wailed. 'I WANT TO BE ON *GROSS-OUT*! I WANT TO BE ON *GROSS-OUT*!'

Perfect Peter opened his letter. The sweet smell of lavender wafted out.

Dear Peter,
what a wonderful letter you wrote
on the importance of perfect manners!
As a reward I would like to invite you
to be my special guest on the live
broadcast of MANNERS WITH MAGGIE
next Saturday at TV Centre at 9:00
a.m.

You will be showing the girls and
boys at home how to fold a hankie
perfectly, how to hold a knife and fork
elegantly, and how to eat spaghetti
beautifully with a fork and spoon.

I am very much looking forward to
meeting you and to enjoying your lovely
manners in person.

Sincerely,
Maggie.

'I've been invited to appear on *Manners With Maggie*!' said Peter, beaming.

'That's wonderful, Peter!' said Mum. She hugged him.

'I'm so proud of you,' said Dad. He hugged him.

Horrid Henry stopped screaming.

'That's not fair!' said Henry. 'If Peter can be on his favourite TV show why can't I be on mine?'

Mum and Dad looked at each other.

'I suppose he does have a point,' said Dad. He sighed.

'And we don't have to tell anyone he's on,' said Mum. She sighed.

'All right, Henry. You can be a contestant.'

'YIPPEE!' squealed Henry, stomping on the sofa and doing his victory jig. 'I'm going to be a star! *Gross-Out* here I come!'

The great day arrived at last. Horrid Henry had been practising so hard with his Goo-Shooter he could hit Perfect Peter's nose at thirty paces. He'd also been practising shovelling ice cream into his mouth as fast as he could, until Mum caught him.

Perfect Peter had been practising so hard folding his hankie that he could do it with one hand. And no one could twirl spaghetti with a spoon as beautifully or hold a knife and fork as elegantly as Perfect Peter.

At nine a.m. sharp, Mum, Henry, and Peter walked into TV Centre. Henry was starving. He'd skipped breakfast, to have more room for all the ice cream he'd be gobbling.

Horrid Henry wore old jeans and dirty trainers. Perfect Peter wore a jacket and tie.

A woman with red hair and freckles rushed up to them with a clipboard.

'Hi, I'm Super Sally. Welcome to TV Centre. I'm sorry boys, we'll have to dash, we're running late. Come with me to the guests' waiting room. You're both on in five minutes.'

'Can't I stay with them?' said Mum.

'Parents to remain downstairs in the parents' room,' said Super Sally sternly. 'You can watch on the monitors there.'

'Good luck, boys,' said Mum, waving.

Sally stared at Peter as they hurried down the hall.

'Aren't you worried about getting those smart clothes dirty?' said Sally.

Peter looked shocked.

'I never get my clothes dirty,' he said.

'There's always a first time,' chortled Sally. 'Here's the waiting room. Studios one and two where you'll be filming are through those doors at the end.'

In the room was a sofa and two tables. One, marked *Gross-Out*, was groaning with sweets, crisps and fizzy drinks.

The second, labelled *Manners with Maggie*, was laid with a crisp white cloth. A few dainty vegetables were displayed on a china plate.

Horrid Henry suddenly felt nervous. Today was his day to be a TV star! Had he practised enough? And he was so hungry! His stomach tightened.

'I need a wee,' said Horrid Henry.

'Toilets next door,' said Super Sally. 'Be quick. You're on in one minute.'

Perfect Peter didn't feel in the least nervous. Practice made perfect, and he knew he was. What disgusting food, he thought, wandering over to the *Gross-Out* table.

A man wearing combat fatigues dashed into the room.

'Ah, there you are!' he boomed. 'Come along! It's your big moment!'

'I'm ready,' said Peter, waving his handkerchief.

The man pushed him through the door marked Stage 1.

Henry returned.

A lady in high heels and a pearl necklace poked her head round the door.

'You're on, dear!' said the lady. 'Goodness, you look a little untidy. Never mind, can't be helped.' And she ushered Henry through the door marked Stage 2.

Henry found himself on a brightly lit stage. He blinked in the brilliant lights.

'Let's give a warm welcome to today's guest!' cried a voice. A *female* voice.

The studio audience exploded into applause.

Henry froze. Who was that woman?

Where was Marvin the Maniac?

Something's wrong, he thought. This was not the set of *Gross-Out*. It was a pink and yellow kitchen. Yet it looked vaguely familiar . . .

Meanwhile, on Stage 1, Perfect Peter shrank back in horror as two gigantic children carrying Goo-Shooters and massive bowls of ice cream advanced towards him. A presenter, laughing like a hyena, egged them on.

'You're not Maggie!' said Peter. 'And I don't know how to use a—'

'Get him guys!' squealed Marvin the Maniac.

'HELLLLP!' shrieked Peter.

Back on Stage 2, Henry suddenly realised where he was.

'Now don't be shy, darling!' said the presenter, walking quickly to Henry and taking him firmly by the hand. 'Peter's here to show us how to fold a hankie and how to eat beautifully!' It was Maggie. From *Manners with Maggie*.

What could Henry do? He was on live TV! There were the cameras zooming in on him. If he screamed there'd been a terrible mistake that would ruin the

show. And hadn't he heard that the show must go on? Even a dreadful show like *Manners with Maggie*?

Henry strolled onto centre stage, smiling and bowing.

'Now Peter will show us the perfect way to fold a hankie.'

Horrid Henry felt a sneeze coming.

'AAAACHOOO!' he sneezed. Then he wiped his nose on his sleeve.

The audience giggled. Maggie looked stunned.

'The . . . hankie,' she prompted.

'Oh yeah,' said Henry, feeling in his pockets. He removed

a few crumpled wads of ancient tissue.

'Here, use mine,' said Maggie smoothly.

Henry took the beautifully embroidered square of silky cloth and scrunched it into a ball. Then he stuffed it into his pocket.

'Nothing to it,' said Henry. 'Scrunch and stuff. But why bother with a hankie when a sleeve works so much better?'

Maggie gulped. 'Very funny, Peter dear! We know he's only joking, don't we, children! Now we'll show the girls and boys—'

But Horrid Henry had noticed the table, set with a chocolate cake and a large bowl of spaghetti. Yummy! And Henry hadn't eaten anything for ages.

'Hey, that cake looks great!' interrupted Henry. He dashed to the table, dug out a nice big hunk and shoved it in his mouth.

'Stop eating!' hissed Maggie. 'We haven't finished the hankie demonstration yet!'

But Henry didn't stop.

'Yummy,' he said, licking his fingers.

Maggie looked like she was going to faint.

'Show the girls and boys how to use a knife and fork elegantly, Peter,' she said, with gritted teeth.

'Nah, a knife and fork slows you down too much. I *always* eat with my fingers. See?'

Horrid Henry waved his chocolate-covered hands.

'I'm sure it was just the excitement of being on TV that made you forget to offer me a slice of cake,' prompted Maggie. She gazed in horror at the cake, now with a gaping hole on the side.

'But I want to eat it all myself!' said Horrid Henry. 'I'm starving! Get your own cake.'

'Now I'm going to teach you the proper way to eat spaghetti,' said Maggie stiffly, pretending she hadn't heard. 'Which we should have done first, of course, as we do not eat dessert before the main course.'

'I do!' said Henry.

'Hold your spoon in your left hand, fork in your right, pick up a teensy tiny amount of spaghetti and twirl twirl twirl. Let's see if my little helper can do it. I'm sure he's been practising at home.'

''Course,' lied Henry. How hard could it be to twirl spaghetti? Henry picked up his spoon, plunged his fork into an enormous pile of spaghetti and started to twirl. The spaghetti flew round the kitchen. A few

strands landed on Maggie's head.

'Whoops,' said Henry. 'I'll try again.' Before Maggie could stop him he'd seized another huge forkful.

'It keeps falling off,' said Henry. 'Listen, kids, use your fingers – it's faster.' Then Henry scooped a handful of spaghetti and crammed it into his mouth.

'It's good,' mumbled Henry, chewing loudly with his mouth open.

'Stop! Stop!' said Maggie. Her voice rose to a polite scream.

'What's wrong?' said Henry, trailing great strings of spaghetti out of his mouth.

Suddenly Henry heard a high-pitched howl. Then Perfect Peter burst onto the set, covered in green goo, followed by whooping children waving Goo-Shooters.

'Maggie! Save me!' shrieked Peter, dropping his shooter and hurling himself into her arms. 'They're trying to make me eat between meals!'

'Get away from me, you horrible child!' screamed Maggie.

It was the Goo-Shooter gang at last! Better late than never, thought Henry.

'Yeee haaa!' Henry snatched Peter's Goo-Shooter, jumped onto the table and sprayed Tapioca Tina, Tank

Thomas and most of the audience. Gleefully, they returned fire. Henry took a step back, and stepped into the spaghetti.

SPLAT!

'Help!' screamed Maggie, green goo and spaghetti dripping from her face.

'Help!' screamed Peter, green goo and spaghetti dripping from his hair.

'CUT!' shouted the director.

Horrid Henry was lying on the comfy black chair flicking channels. Sadly, *Manners with Maggie* was no longer on TV since Maggie had been dragged screaming off the set. *Mischief with Mildred* would be on soon. Henry thought he'd give it a try.

Hey TV people:

Now that you've dumped Manners with Maggie, I've got a great idea: Manners with **Henry**! This would be such more fun. I would show everyone how to slurp spaghetti; how to chew with their mouth open; the fastest way to eat with your fingers; how to slouch and eat; why you should never use a fork again; 10 tips for belching; and why you should never say please or thank you.

From

Henry

HORRiD HENRY'S
Revenge

SLAP!

'Waaaaaaaaaa!'

SLAP! SLAP! PINCH!

'Muuuummmmmm!' shrieked Peter. 'Henry slapped me!'

'Did not!'

'Did too! And he pinched me!'

'Stop being horrid, Henry!' said Mum.

'But Peter started it!' shouted Henry.

'Did not!' wailed Peter. 'Henry did!'

Horrid Henry glared at Perfect Peter.

Perfect Peter glared at Horrid Henry.

Mum went back to writing her letter. Horrid Henry lashed out and pulled Peter's hair. He was a coiling cobra unleashing his venom.

'**E**owwwwww!' shrieked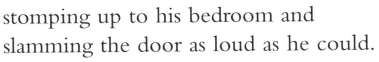
Peter.

'Go to your room, Henry!' screamed Dad. 'I've had just about enough of you today!'

'Fine!' shouted Henry. 'I hate you, Peter!' he shrieked, stomping up to his bedroom and slamming the door as loud as he could.

It was so unfair! Peter was never sent to his room. Horrid Henry was sent to his so often he might as well live there full-time. Henry couldn't burp without Peter trying to get him into trouble.

'Mum! Henry's dropping peas on the floor!'

'Dad! Henry's sneaking sweets!'

'Mum! Henry's eating on the new sofa!'

'Dad! Henry's playing on the phone!'

Horrid Henry had had enough. He was sick and tired of that goody-goody ugly toad tattle-tale brat.

But what could he do about Peter? He'd tried selling him as a slave to Moody Margaret, but Henry didn't think she'd buy him again. If only he knew how to cast spells, he could turn Peter into a toad or a beetle or a worm. Yes! Wouldn't that be great! He'd charge everyone 10p to look at his brother, the worm. And if Peter-worm ever wriggled out of line he'd be fish bait. Horrid Henry smiled.

Then he sighed. The truth was, he was stuck with Peter. But if he couldn't sell Peter, and he couldn't turn Peter into a worm, he could get Peter into trouble.

Unfortunately, getting Perfect Peter into trouble was easier said than done. Peter never did anything wrong. Also, for some reason he didn't always trust Henry. The only way to get Peter into trouble was to trick him. And if it took all year, Horrid Henry vowed he would come up with a perfect plan. A plan to get Peter into trouble. Big, big, BIG trouble. That would be almost as good as turning him into a worm.

'I'll pay you back, Peter,' growled Henry, thumping his teddy, Mr Kill, against the bedpost. 'I will be revenged on you!'

'What are you doing, Henry?' asked Peter.

'Nothing,' said Horrid Henry. Quickly he stopped poking around the old apple tree at the end of the garden and stood up.

'You're doing something, I know you are,' said Peter.

'Whatever I'm doing is none of your business, telltale,' said Henry.

'Have you found something?' said Peter. He looked at the base of the tree. 'I don't see anything.'

'Maybe,' said Henry. 'But I'm not telling you. You can't keep a secret.'

'Yes I can,' said Peter.

'And you're too young,' said Henry.

'No I'm not,' said Peter. 'I'm a big boy. Mum said so.'

'Well, too bad,' said Horrid Henry. 'Now go away and leave me alone. I'm doing something important.'

Perfect Peter slunk off about ten paces, then turned and stood still, watching Henry.

Horrid Henry continued to prowl around the tree, staring intently at the grass. Then he whistled and dropped to his knees.

'What have you found?' said Perfect Peter eagerly. 'Treasure?'

'Much better than treasure,' said Horrid Henry. He picked something up and hid it in his hand.

'Oh show me,' said Peter. 'Please. Oh please!'

Horrid Henry considered.

'If – and I mean if – I tell you something, do you swear by the sacred oath of the Purple Hand to say nothing about this to anyone?'

'I swear,' said Peter.

'Even if you're being tortured by aliens?'

'I WON'T TELL!' shrieked Peter.

Horrid Henry put his finger to his lips, then tiptoed away from the tree to his fort. Peter followed.

'I don't want them to know I'm telling you,' he whispered, when they were hidden behind the branches. 'Otherwise they'll disappear.'

'Who?' whispered Peter.

'The fairies,' said Henry.

'Fairies,' squeaked Perfect Peter. 'You mean you've seen—'

'Shh!' hissed Horrid Henry. 'They'll run away if you tell anyone.'

'I won't,' said Perfect Peter. 'Promise.

Oh wow, fairies! In our garden! Oh, Henry! Fairies! Just wait till I tell my teacher.'

'NO!' screamed Horrid Henry. 'Tell no one. Especially grown-ups. Fairies hate grown-ups. Grown-ups stink to fairies.'

Perfect Peter clasped his hand over his mouth.

'Sorry, Henry,' he said.

Horrid Henry opened his hand. It was sprinkled with gold glitter.

'Fairy dust,' said Horrid Henry.

'It looks just like glitter,' said Perfect Peter.

'Of course it looks like glitter,' said Horrid Henry. 'Where do you think glitter comes from?'

'Wow,' said Peter. 'I never knew glitter came from fairies.'

'Well now you know,' said Henry.

'Can I see them, Henry?' asked Peter. 'Please let me see them!'

'They only come out to dance at dead of night,' said Horrid Henry.

'Past my bedtime?' said Perfect Peter.

'Course,' said Horrid Henry. 'Midnight is the fairy hour.'

'Oh,' said Peter. His face fell.

'Told you you were too young,' said Henry.

'Wait,' said Perfect Peter. 'If they only come out at midnight, how come you've seen them?'

'Because I've sneaked out and hidden up the apple tree,' said Horrid Henry. 'It's the only way.'

'Ah,' said Perfect Peter. 'Umm,' said Perfect Peter. 'Ooh,' said Perfect Peter.

'I'm going to see them tonight,' said Henry casually.

'Do you think you could ask them to come before seven-thirty?' said Peter.

'Oh yeah, right,' said Henry. '"Hiya, fairies! My brother wants you to dance for him at seven o'clock." "Sure thing, Henry,"' said Henry in a high squeaky fairy voice. 'You don't speak to fairies. You have to hide up the tree. If they knew I'd seen them they'd run away and never come back.'

Perfect Peter was in torment. He wanted to see the fairies more than anything in the world. But getting

257

out of bed after lights out! And sneaking outside! And climbing the tree! And on a school night! It was too much.

'I can't do it,' whispered Perfect Peter.

Henry shrugged. 'Fine, baby. You need your rest.'

Peter hated being called baby. Next to 'smelly nappy', it was the worst name Henry could call him.

'I am not a baby.'

'Yes you are,' said Henry. 'Now go away, baby. Just don't blame me when you spend the rest of your life moaning that you missed seeing real live fairies.'

Horrid Henry started to leave the fort.

Perfect Peter sat very still. Fairies! But was he brave enough, and bad enough, to sneak out of the house – at night?

'Don't do it,' whispered his angel.

'Do it,' squeaked his devil, a very small, sad, puny creature who spent his life inside Peter's head squashed flat by the angel.

'I'll come,' said Perfect Peter.
YES! thought Horrid Henry.
'Okay,' said Henry.

Tiptoe. Tiptoe.
        Tiptoe. Tiptoe.
            Tiptoe. Tiptoe.

Horrid Henry sneaked down the stairs. Perfect Peter followed him. Softly, Henry opened the back door, and slipped outside. He held a small torch.

'It's so dark!' said Perfect Peter, staring into the shadows at the bottom of the garden.

'Quiet,' whispered Horrid Henry. 'Follow me.'

They crept across the lawn down to the apple tree. Perfect Peter looked up into the ghostly branches.

'It's too high for me to climb,' he protested.

'No it isn't, I'll give you a leg up,' said Horrid Henry. He grabbed Peter and shoved him up. Peter caught the lowest branch and started to climb.

'Higher,' said Henry. 'Go as high as you can.'

Peter climbed. And climbed. And climbed.

'This is high enough,' squeaked Perfect Peter. He settled himself on a branch, then cautiously looked down. 'I don't see anything,' he whispered.

There was no reply.

'Henry?' said Peter.

'Henry!' said Peter, a little louder.

Still there was no reply. Perfect Peter peered into the darkness. Where could he be? Could Henry have been kidnapped by fairies? Oh no!

Then Perfect Peter saw a dreadful sight.

There was his brother, darting back into the house!

Perfect Peter did not understand. Why wasn't Henry waiting to see the fairies? Why had he left Peter?

And then suddenly Peter realised the terrible truth. His treacherous brother had tricked him.

'I'll get you – you're gonna be in big trouble – I'll – I'll— ' squeaked Peter. Then he stopped. His legs were too short to reach the lower branch.

Perfect Peter couldn't climb down. He was stuck up a tree, all alone, at night. He had three choices. He could wait and hope that Henry would come back and help him. Fat chance. Or he could sleep all night in the damp, cold, scary, spooky tree. Or he could—

'MUUUUUUUM!' screamed Peter. 'DAAAADD!'

Mum and Dad stumbled out into the darkness. They were furious.

'What are you doing out here, Peter!' screamed Mum.

'You horrible boy!' screamed Dad.

'It was Henry's fault!' shrieked Peter, as Dad helped him down. 'He brought me here! He made me climb up.'

'Henry is sound asleep in bed,' said Mum. 'We checked on the way out.'

'I am so disappointed in you, Peter,' said Dad. 'No stamp collecting for a month.'

'WAAAAAAAH!' wailed Peter.

'Shuddup!' screamed the neighbours. 'We're trying to sleep.'

Meanwhile, back in bed, Horrid Henry stretched and smiled. No one could pretend to be asleep better than Horrid Henry.

What a perfect revenge, he thought. Peter in trouble. Henry in the clear. He was so excited he never noticed his torn, dirty, leafy clothes.

Unfortunately, the next morning, Mum did.

Perfect Peter's Top Secret Fairy Notes

What to do when you meet a fairy

1. Fairies are shy, so always whisper
2. Walk on tiptoe
3. Dress up as one yourself
4. Cover yourself in glitter
5. Choose a fairy name for yourself like Blossom

Remember,
Fairy Liquid is not for fairies!

HORRID HENRY'S
Wedding

'm not wearing these horrible clothes and that's that!'

Horrid Henry glared at the mirror. A stranger smothered in a lilac ruffled shirt, green satin knickerbockers, tights, pink cummerbund tied in a floppy bow and pointy white satin shoes with gold buckles glared back at him.

Henry had never seen anyone looking so silly in his life.

'Aha ha ha ha ha!' shrieked Horrid Henry, pointing at the mirror.

Then Henry peered more closely. The ridiculous-looking boy was him.

Perfect Peter stood next to Horrid Henry. He too was smothered in a lilac ruffled shirt, green satin knickerbockers, tights, pink cummerbund and pointy white shoes with gold buckles. But unlike Henry, Peter was smiling.

'Aren't they adorable?' squealed Prissy Polly. 'That's how my children are always going to dress.'

Prissy Polly was Horrid Henry's horrible older cousin. Prissy Polly was always squeaking and squealing:

'Eeek, it's a speck of dust.'

'Eeek, it's a puddle.'

'Eeek, my hair is a mess.'

But when Prissy Polly announced she was getting married to Pimply Paul and wanted Henry and Peter to be pageboys, Mum said yes before Henry could stop her.

'What's a pageboy?' asked Henry suspiciously.

'A pageboy carries the wedding rings down the aisle on a satin cushion,' said Mum.

'And throws confetti afterwards,' said Dad.

Henry liked the idea of throwing confetti. But carrying rings on a cushion? No thanks.

'I don't want to be a pageboy,' said Henry.

'I do, I do,' said Peter.

'You're going to be a pageboy, and that's that,' said Mum.

'And you'll behave yourself,' said Dad. 'It's very kind of cousin Polly to ask you.'

Henry scowled.

'Who'd want to be married to *her*?' said Henry. 'I wouldn't if you paid me a million pounds.'

But for some reason the bridegroom, Pimply Paul, did want to marry Prissy Polly. And as far as Henry knew, he had not been paid one million pounds.

Pimply Paul was also trying on his wedding clothes. He looked ridiculous in a black top hat, lilac shirt, and a black jacket covered in gold swirls.

'I won't wear these silly clothes,' said Henry.

'Oh be quiet, you little brat,' snapped Pimply Paul.

Horrid Henry glared at him.

'I won't,' said Henry. 'And that's final.'

'Henry, stop being horrid,' said Mum. She looked

extremely silly in a big
floppy hat dripping
with flowers.

Suddenly
Henry grabbed at
the lace ruffles round
his throat.

'I'm choking,' he
gasped. 'I can't breathe.'

Then Henry fell to the
floor and rolled around.

'Uggggghhhhhhh,' moaned
Henry. 'I'm dying.'

'Get up this minute, Henry!' said Dad.

'Eeek, there's dirt on the floor!' shrieked Polly.

'Can't you control that child?' hissed Pimply Paul.

'I DON'T WANT TO BE A PAGEBOY!' howled Horrid Henry.

'Thank you so much for asking me to be a pageboy, Polly,' shouted Perfect Peter, trying to be heard over Henry's screams.

'You're welcome,' shouted Polly.

'Stop that, Henry!' ordered Mum. 'I've never been so ashamed in my life.'

'I hate children,' muttered Pimply Paul under his breath.

Horrid Henry stopped. Unfortunately, his pageboy clothes looked as fresh and crisp as ever.

All right, thought Horrid Henry. You want me at the wedding? You've got me.

Prissy Polly's wedding day arrived. Henry was delighted to see rain pouring down. How cross Polly would be.

Perfect Peter was already dressed.

'Isn't this going to be fun, Henry?' said Peter.

'No!' said Henry, sitting on the floor. 'And I'm not going.'

Mum and Dad stuffed Henry into his pageboy clothes. It was hard, heavy work.

Finally everyone was in the car.

'We're going to be late!' shrieked Mum.

'We're going to be late!' shrieked Dad.

'We're going to be late!' shrieked Perfect Peter.

'Good!' muttered Henry.

Mum, Dad, Henry and Peter arrived at the church. Boom! There was a clap of thunder. Rain poured down. All the other guests were already inside.

'Watch out for the puddle, boys,' said Mum, as she leapt out of the car. She opened her umbrella.

Dad jumped
over the puddle.

Peter jumped over the puddle.

Henry jumped over the
puddle, and tripped.

SPLASH!

'Oopsy,' said Henry.

His ruffles were torn, his
knickerbockers were filthy,
and his satin shoes were
soaked.

Mum, Dad and
Peter were covered in muddy water.

Perfect Peter burst into tears.

'You've ruined my
pageboy clothes,'
sobbed Peter.

Mum
wiped as much
dirt as she
could off Henry
and Peter.

272

'It was an accident, Mum, really,' said Henry.

'Hurry up, you're late!' shouted Pimply Paul.

Mum and Dad dashed into the church. Henry and Peter stayed outside, waiting to make their entrance.

Pimply Paul and his best man, Cross Colin, stared at Henry and Peter.

'You look a mess,' said Paul.

'It was an accident,' said Henry.

Peter snivelled.

'Now be careful with the wedding rings,' said Cross Colin. He handed Henry and Peter a satin cushion each, with a gold ring on top.

A great quivering lump of lace and taffeta and bows and flowers approached. Henry guessed Prissy Polly must be lurking somewhere underneath.

'Eeek,' squeaked the clump. 'Why did it have to rain on my wedding?'

'Eeek,' squeaked the clump again. 'You're filthy.'

Perfect Peter began to sob. The satin cushion trembled in his hand. The ring balanced precariously near the edge.

Cross Colin snatched Peter's cushion.

'You can't carry a ring with your hand shaking like that,' snapped Colin. 'You'd better carry them both, Henry.'

'Come *on*,' hissed Pimply Paul. 'We're late!'

Cross Colin and Pimply Paul dashed into the church.

The music started. Henry pranced down the aisle after Polly. Everyone stood up.

Henry beamed and bowed and waved. He was King Henry the Horrible, smiling graciously at his cheering subjects before he chopped off their heads.

As he danced along, he stepped on Polly's long trailing dress.

Riiiip.

'Eeeeek!' squeaked Prissy Polly.

Part of Polly's train lay beneath Henry's muddy satin shoe.

That dress was too long anyway, thought Henry. He picked the fabric out of the way and stomped down the aisle.

The bride, groom, best man, and pageboys assembled in front of the vicar.

Henry stood . . . and stood . . . and stood. The vicar droned on . . . and on . . . and on. Henry's arm holding up the cushion began to ache.

This is boring, thought Henry, jiggling the rings on the cushion.

Boing! Boing! Boing!

Oooh, thought Henry. I'm good at ring tossing.

The rings bounced.

The vicar droned.

Henry was a famous pancake chef, tossing the pancakes higher and higher and higher . . .

Clink clunk.

The rings rolled down the aisle and vanished down a small grate.

Oops, thought Henry.

'May I have the rings, please?' said the minister.

Everyone looked at Henry.

'He's got them,' said Henry desperately, pointing at Peter.

'I have not,' sobbed Peter.

Henry reached into his pocket. He found two pieces of old chewing-gum, some gravel, and his lucky pirate ring.

'Here, use this,' he said.

At last, Pimply Paul and Prissy Polly were married.

Cross Colin handed Henry and Peter a basket of pink and yellow rose petals each.

'Throw the petals in front of the bride and groom

as they walk back down the aisle,' whispered Colin.

'I will,' said Peter. He scattered the petals before Pimply Paul and Prissy Polly.

'So will I,' said Henry. He hurled a handful of petals in Pimply Paul's face.

'Watch it, you little brat,' snarled Paul.

'Windy, isn't it?' said Henry. He hurled another handful of petals at Polly.

'Eeek,' squeaked Prissy Polly.

'Everyone outside for photographs,' said the photographer.

Horrid Henry loved having his picture taken. He dashed out.

'Pictures of the bride and groom first,' said the photographer.

Henry jumped in front.

Click.

Henry peeked from the side.

Click.

Henry stuck out his tongue.

Click.

Henry made horrible rude faces. **Click.**

'This way to the reception!' said Cross Colin. The wedding party was held in a nearby hotel.

The adults did nothing but talk and eat, talk and drink, talk and eat. Perfect Peter sat at the table and ate his lunch.

Horrid Henry sat under the table and poked people's legs. He crawled around and squashed some toes. Then Henry got bored and drifted into the next room.

There was the wedding cake, standing alone, on a table. It was the most delicious-looking cake Henry had ever seen. It had three layers and was covered in luscious white icing and yummy iced flowers and bells and leaves.

Henry's mouth watered.

I'll just taste a teeny weeny bit of petal, thought Henry. No harm in that.

He broke off a morsel and popped it in his mouth.

Hmmmmm boy! That icing tasted great.

Perhaps just one more bite, thought Henry. If I take it from the back, no one will notice.

Henry carefully selected an icing rose from the bottom tier and stuffed it in his mouth. Wow.

Henry stood back from the case. It looked a little uneven now, with that rose missing from the bottom.

I'll just even it up, thought Henry. It was the work of a moment to break off a rose from the middle tier and another from the top.

Then a strange thing happened.

'Eat me,' whispered the cake. 'Go on.'

Who was Henry to ignore such a request?

He picked out a few crumbs from the back.

Delicious, thought Henry. Then he took a few more. And a few more. Then he dug out a nice big chunk.

'What do you think you're doing?' shouted Pimply Paul.

Henry ran round the cake table. Paul ran after him. Round and round and round the cake they ran.

'Just wait till I get my hands on you!' snarled Pimply Paul.

Henry dashed under the table.
Pimply Paul lunged for him and missed.

SPLAT.

Pimply Paul fell head first on to the cake.
Henry slipped away.

Prissy Polly ran into the room.

'Eeek,' she shrieked.

'Wasn't that a lovely wedding,' sighed Mum on the way home. 'Funny they didn't have a cake, though.'

'Oh yes,' said Dad.

'Oh yes,' said Peter.

'OH YES!' said Henry. 'I'll be glad to be a pageboy any time.'

Dear Cousins,

Paul and I are sorry to have taken so long to send this thank you letter for the lovely toaster you gave us, but it has taken a while to recover from our eventful wedding. When Paul fell onto the cake he hurt his nose and the bandages have only just come off.

I suppose most pageboys lose the rings and throw rose petals at the bride instead of in front of her and fall into puddles and ruin their very expensive pageboy outfits that the bride and groom have paid for and step on the bride's dress and rip it though I have yet to meet one.

As Henry managed to get himself into all of our wedding pictures, we won't be forgetting him in a hurry. If you would like any copies we would happily send you a set.

Love from your cousins,
Polly and Paul

P.S. we've enclosed Henry's pirate ring.

HORRID HENRY'S Hike

Horrid Henry looked out of the window.
HAAARRRGGGHHH! It was a lovely day.
The sun was shining. The birds were tweeting.
The breeze was blowing. Little fluffy clouds floated by
in a bright blue sky.

Rats.

Why couldn't it be raining? Or hailing? Or
sleeting?

Any minute, any second, it would happen…the
words he'd been dreading, the words he'd give
anything not to hear, the words –

'Henry! Peter! Time to go for a walk,' called Mum.

'Yippee!' said Perfect Peter. 'I can wear my new
yellow wellies!'

'NO!' screamed Horrid Henry.

Go for a walk! Go for a walk! Didn't he walk enough already? He walked to school. He walked home from school. He walked to the TV. He walked to the computer. He walked to the sweet jar *and* all the way back to the comfy black chair. Horrid Henry walked plenty. Ugghh. The last thing he needed was more walking. More chocolate, yes. More crisps, yes. More *walking*? No way! Why oh why couldn't his parents ever say, 'Henry! Time to play on the computer.' Or 'Henry, stop doing your homework this minute! Time to turn on the TV.'

But no. For some reason his mean, horrible parents thought he spent too much time sitting indoors. They'd been threatening for weeks to make him go on a family walk. Now the dreadful moment had come. His precious weekend was ruined.

Horrid Henry hated nature. Horrid Henry hated fresh air. What could be more boring than walking up and down streets staring at lamp posts? Or sloshing across some stupid muddy park? Nature smelled. Uggh! He'd much rather be inside watching TV.

Mum stomped into the sitting room.

'Henry! Didn't you hear me calling?'

'No,' lied Henry.

'Get your wellies on, we're going,' said Dad, rubbing his hands. 'What a lovely day.'

'I don't want to go for a walk,' said Henry. 'I want to watch *Rapper Zapper Zaps Terminator Gladiator*.'

'But Henry,' said Perfect Peter, 'fresh air and exercise are so good for you.'

'I don't care!' shrieked Henry.

Horrid Henry stomped downstairs and flung open the front door. He breathed in deeply, hopped on one foot, then shut the door.

'There! Done it. Fresh air *and* exercise,' snarled Henry.

'Henry, we're going,' said Mum. 'Get in the car.'

Henry's ears pricked up.

'The car?' said Henry. 'I thought we were going for a walk.'

'We are,' said Mum. 'In the countryside.'

'Hurray!' said Perfect Peter. 'A nice *long* walk.'

'NOOOO!' howled Henry. Plodding along in the boring old park was bad enough, with its mouldy leaves and dog poo and stumpy trees. But at least the park wasn't very big. But the *countryside*?

The countryside was enormous! They'd be walking for hours, days, weeks, months, till his legs wore down to stumps and his feet fell off. And the countryside was so dangerous! Horrid Henry was sure he'd be swallowed up by quicksand or trampled to death by marauding chickens.

'I live in the city!' shrieked Henry. 'I don't want to go to the country!'

'Time you got out more,' said Dad.

'But look at those clouds,' moaned Henry, pointing to a fluffy wisp. 'We'll get soaked.'

'A little water never hurt anyone,' said Mum.

Oh yeah? Wouldn't they be sorry when he died of pneumonia.

'I'm staying here and that's final!' screamed Henry.

'Henry, we're waiting,' said Mum.

'Good,' said Henry.

'*I'm* all ready, Mum,' said Peter.

'I'm going to start deducting pocket money,' said Dad. '5p, 10p, 15p, 20— '

Horrid Henry pulled on his wellies, stomped out of the door and got in the car. He slammed the door as hard as he could. It was so unfair! Why did he never get to do what *he* wanted to do? Now he would miss the first time Rapper Zapper had ever slugged it out with Terminator Gladiator. And all because he had to go on a long, boring, exhausting, horrible hike. He was so miserable he didn't even have the energy to kick Peter.

'Can't we just walk round the block?' moaned Henry.

'N-O spells no,' said Dad. 'We're going for a lovely walk in the countryside and that's that.'

Horrid Henry slumped miserably in his seat. Boy would they be sorry when he was gobbled up by goats. Boo hoo, if only we hadn't gone on that walk in the wilds, Mum would wail. Henry was right, we should have listened to him, Dad would sob.

I miss Henry, Peter would howl. I'll never eat goat's cheese again. And now it's too late, they would shriek.

If only, thought Horrid Henry. That would serve them right.

All too soon, Mum pulled into a car park, on the edge of a small wood.

'Wow,' said Perfect Peter. 'Look at all those lovely trees.'

'Bet there are werewolves hiding there,' muttered Henry. 'And I hope they come and eat you!'

'Mum!' squealed Peter. 'Henry's trying to scare me.'

'Don't be horrid, Henry,' said Mum.

Horrid Henry looked around him. There was a gate, leading to endless meadows bordered by

hedgerows. A muddy path wound through the trees and across the fields. A church spire stuck up in the distance.

'Right, I've seen the countryside, let's go home,' said Henry.

Mum glared at him.

'What?' said Henry, scowling.

'Let's enjoy this lovely day,' said Dad, sighing.

'So what do we do now?' said Henry.

'Walk,' said Dad.

'Where?' said Henry.

'Just walk,' said Mum, 'and enjoy the beautiful scenery.'

Henry groaned.

'We're heading for the lake,' said Dad, striding off. 'I've brought bread and we can feed the ducks.'

'But *Rapper Zapper* starts in an hour!'

'Tough,' said Mum.

Mum, Dad, and Peter headed through the gate into the field. Horrid Henry trailed behind them walking as slowly as he could.

'Ahh, breathe the lovely fresh air,' said Mum.

'We should do this more often,' said Dad.

Henry sniffed.

The horrible smell of manure filled his nostrils.

'Ewww, smelly,' said Henry. 'Peter, couldn't you wait?'

'MUM!' shrieked Peter. 'Henry called me smelly.'

'Did not!'

'Did too!'

'Did not, smelly.'

'WAAAAAAAAA!' wailed Peter. 'Tell him to stop!'

'Don't be horrid, Henry!' screamed Mum. Her voice echoed. A dog walker passed her, and glared.

'Peter, would you rather run a mile, jump a stile, or eat a country pancake?' said Henry sweetly.

'Ooh,' said Peter. 'I love pancakes. And a country one must be even more delicious than a city one.'

'Ha ha,' cackled Horrid Henry, sticking out his tongue. 'Fooled you. Peter wants to eat cowpats!'

'MUM!' screamed Peter.

Henry walked.

   And walked.

         And walked.

His legs felt heavier, and heavier, and heavier.

'This field is muddy,' moaned Henry.

'I'm bored,' groaned Henry.

'My feet hurt,' whined Henry.

'Can't we go home? We've already walked miles,' whinged Henry.

'We've been walking for ten minutes,' said Dad.

'Please can we go on walks more often,' said Perfect Peter. 'Oh, look at those fluffy little sheepies!'

Horrid Henry pounced. He was a zombie biting the head off the hapless human.

'AAAAEEEEEE!' squealed Peter.

'Henry!' screamed Mum.

'Stop it!' screamed Dad. 'Or no TV for a week.'

When he was king, thought Horrid Henry, any parent who made their children go on a hike would be dumped barefoot in a scorpion-infested desert.

Plod.

Plod.

Plod.

Horrid Henry dragged his feet. Maybe his horrible mean parents would get fed up waiting for him and turn back, he thought, kicking some mouldy leaves. Squelch.

Squelch.

Squelch.

Oh no, not *another* muddy meadow.

And then suddenly Horrid Henry had an idea. What was he thinking? All that fresh air must be rotting his brain. The sooner they got to the stupid lake, the sooner they could get home for the *Rapper Zapper Zaps Terminator Gladiator*.

'Come on, everyone, let's run!' shrieked Henry. 'Race you down the hill to the lake!'

'That's the spirit, Henry,' said Dad.

Horrid Henry dashed past Dad.

'OW!' shrieked Dad, tumbling into the stinging nettles.

Horrid Henry whizzed past Mum.

'Eww!' shrieked Mum, slipping in a cowpat.

Splat!

Horrid Henry pushed past Peter.
'Waaa!' wailed Peter. 'My wellies
are getting dirty.'
Horrid Henry scampered
down the muddy path.
'Wait Henry!' yelped Mum. 'It's
too slipp – **aaaiiieeeee!**'
Mum slid down
the path on her
bottom.
'Slow
down!'
puffed
Dad.

'I can't run that fast,'
wailed Peter.
But Horrid
Henry raced on.
'Shortcut
across the
field!'
he
called.

'Come on slowcoaches!'

The black and white cow grazing alone in the middle raised its head.

'Henry!' shouted Dad.

Horrid Henry kept running.

'I don't think that's a cow!' shouted Mum.

The cow lowered its head and charged.

'It's a bull!' yelped Mum and Dad. 'RUN!'

'I said it was dangerous in the countryside!' gasped Henry, as everyone clambered over the stile in the nick of time. 'Look, there's the lake!' he added, pointing.

Henry ran down to the water's edge. Peter followed. The embankment narrowed to a point. Peter slipped past Henry and bagged the best spot, right at the water's edge where the ducks gathered.

'Hey, get away from there,' said Henry.

296

'I want to feed the
ducks,' said Peter.

'I want to feed the
ducks,' said Henry.
'Now move.'

'I was here first,'
said Peter.

'Not any more,'
said Henry.

Horrid Henry pushed Peter.

'Out of my way, worm!'

Perfect Peter pushed him back.

'Don't call me worm!'

Henry wobbled.

Peter wobbled.

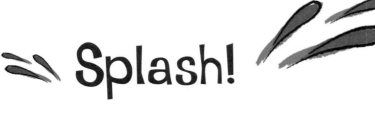 

Splash!

Peter tumbled into the lake.

Crash!

Henry tumbled into the lake.

'My babies!' shrieked Mum, jumping in after them.

'My – glug glug glug!' shrieked Dad, jumping into the muddy water after her.

'My new wellies!' gurgled Perfect Peter.

Bang!

Pow!

Terminator Gladiator slashed at Rapper Zapper.

Zap!

Rapper Zapper slashed back.

'Go Zappy!' yelled Henry, lying bundled up in blankets on the sofa. Once everyone had scrambled out of the lake, Mum and Dad had been keen to get home as fast as possible.

'I think the park next time,' mumbled Dad, sneezing.

'Definitely,' mumbled Mum, coughing.

'Oh, I don't know,' said Horrid Henry happily. 'A little water never hurt anyone.'

Horrid Henry's Nature Guide

Every time you step off a concrete path you are leaving civilisation! The countryside is full of dangers. You will meet:

wild beasts

dangerous paths

swollen rivers

stinging nettles

rampaging chickens

quicksand

horrible smells

mud

zombies

vampires

Beware!
Fresh air.

mummies...

Take it from me – don't leave town. Remember what happened to Hansel and Gretel! It could happen to you! Stay at home and watch TV.

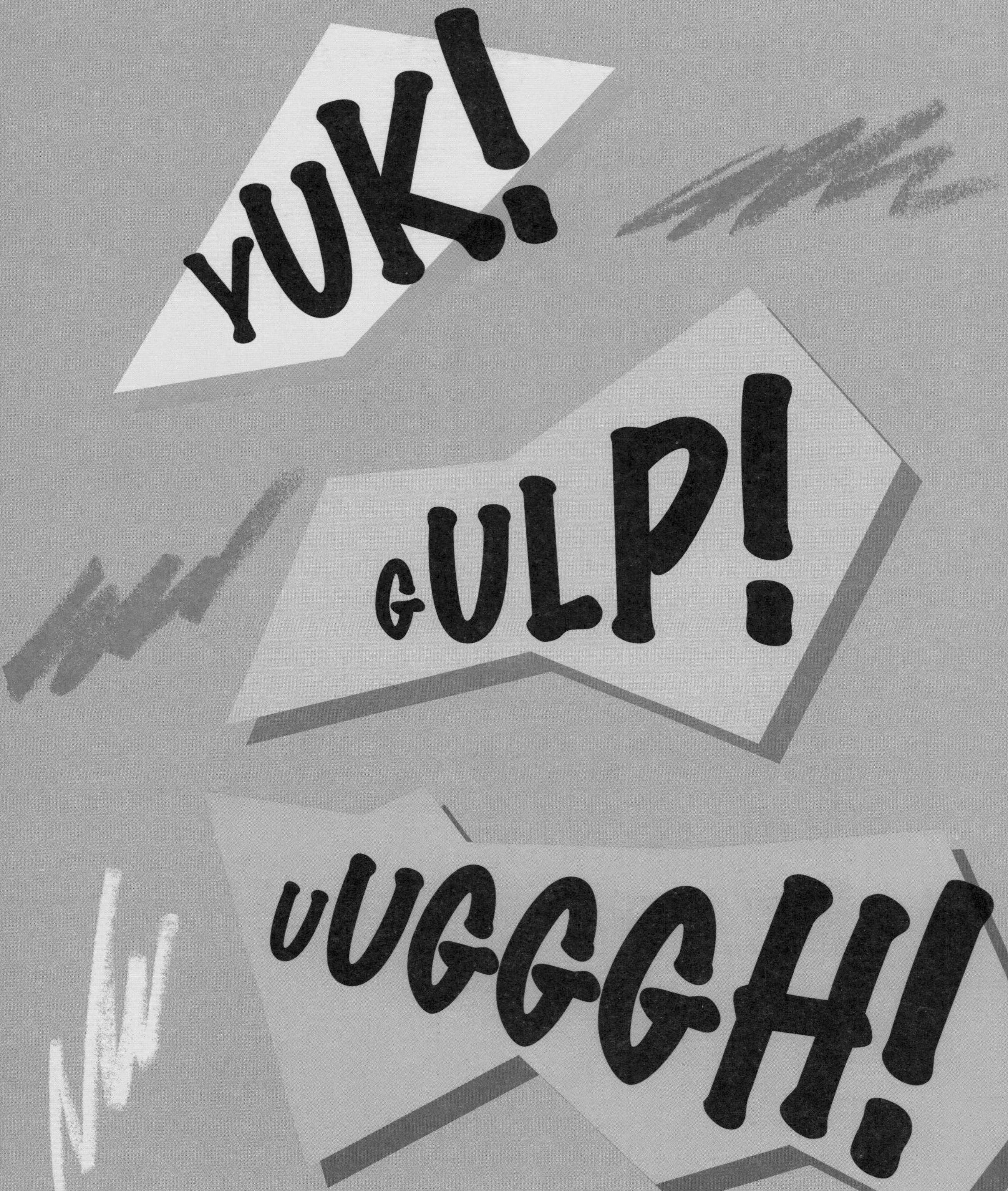
YUK!
GULP!
UGGGH!

HORRID HENRY Dines at Restaurant Le Posh

‘reat news, everyone,’ said Mum, beaming.
‘Aunt Ruby is taking us all out for dinner to
Le Posh, the best French restaurant in town.’

'Oh boy, Restaurant Le Posh,' said Perfect Peter. 'We've never been there.'

Horrid Henry stopped scribbling all over Peter's stamp album. His heart sank. French? Restaurant? Oh no. That meant strange, horrible, yucky food. That meant no burgers, no ketchup, no pizza. That meant –

'**NOOOOOOOOOO!** I don't want to go there!' howled Henry. Who knew what revolting poison would arrive on his plate, covered in gloopy sauce with green bits floating about. **Uggghh**.

'It's Mum's birthday,' said Dad, 'so we're celebrating.'

'I only like Whopper Whoopee,' said Henry. 'Or Fat Frank's. I don't want to go to Le Posh.'

'But Henry,' said Perfect Peter, tidying up his toys, 'it's a chance to try new food.'

Mum beamed. 'Quite right, Peter. It's always nice to try new things.'

'No it isn't,' snarled Horrid Henry. 'I hate trying new food when there's nothing wrong with the old.'

'I love it,' said Dad. 'I eat everything except tomatoes.'

'And I eat everything except squid,' said Mum.

'And I love all vegetables except beetroot,' said Perfect Peter. 'Especially spinach and sprouts.'

'Well I don't,' shrieked Horrid Henry. 'Do they have pasta?'

'Whatever they have will be delicious,' said Mum firmly.

'Do they have burgers? If they don't I'm not going,' wailed Horrid Henry.

Mum looked at Dad.

Dad looked at Mum.

Last time they'd taken Henry to a fancy restaurant he'd had a tantrum under the table. The time before he'd run screaming round the room snatching all the salt and pepper shakers and then thrown up on the people at the next table. The time before that — Mum and Dad preferred not to think about that.

'Shall we get a babysitter?' murmured Dad.

'Leave him home on my birthday?' murmured Mum. She allowed herself to be tempted for a moment. Then she sighed.

'Henry, you are coming and you will be on your best behaviour,' said Mum. 'Your cousin Steve will be there. You wouldn't want Steve to see you make a fuss, would you?'

The hairs on the back of Henry's neck stood up. Steve! Stuck-Up Steve! Horrid Henry's arch-enemy and world's worst cousin. If there was a slimier boy than Steve slithering around then Horrid Henry would eat worms.

Last time they'd met Henry had tricked Steve into thinking there was a monster under his bed. Steve had sworn revenge. There was nothing Steve wouldn't do to get back at Henry.

Boy, did Horrid Henry hate Stuck-Up Steve.

Boy, did Stuck-Up Steve hate Horrid Henry.

'I'm not coming and that's final!' screamed Horrid Henry.

'Henry,' said Dad. 'I'll make a deal with you.'

'What deal?' said Henry. It was always wise to be suspicious when parents offered deals.

'I want you to be pleasant and talk to everyone. And you will eat everything on your plate like everyone else without making a fuss. If you do, I'll give you £2.'

£2! Two whole pounds! Horrid Henry gasped. Two whole pounds just for  talking and shoving a few mouthfuls of disgusting food in his mouth. Normally he had to do that for free.

'How about £3?' said Henry.

'Henry . . .' said Mum.

'OK, deal,' said Horrid Henry. But I won't eat a thing and they can't make me, he thought. He'd find a way. Dad said he had to eat everything on his plate. Well, maybe some food wouldn't stay on his plate. . . Horrid Henry smiled.

Perfect Peter stopped putting away his bricks. He frowned. Shouldn't he get two pounds like Henry?

'What's my reward for being good?' said Perfect Peter.

'Goodness is its own reward,' said Dad.

The restaurant was hushed. The tables were covered in snowy-white tablecloths, with yellow silk chairs. Huge gold chandeliers dangled from the ceiling. Crystal glasses twinkled. The rectangular china plates sparkled. Horrid Henry was impressed.

'Wow,' said Henry. It was like walking into a palace.

'Haven't you ever been here before?' sneered Stuck-Up Steve.

'No,' said Henry.

'*We* eat here all the time,' said Steve. 'I guess you're too poor.'

'It's 'cause *we'd* rather eat at Whopper Whoopee,' lied Henry.

'Hush, Steve,' said Rich Aunt Ruby. 'I'm sure Whopper Whoopee is a lovely restaurant.'

Steve snorted.

Henry kicked him under the table.

'**OWWWW!**' yelped Steve. 'Henry kicked me!'

'No I didn't,' said Henry. 'It was an accident.'

'Henry,' said Mum through gritted teeth. 'Remember what we said about best behaviour? We're in a fancy restaurant.'

Horrid Henry scowled. He looked cautiously around. It was just as he'd feared. Everyone was busy eating weird bits of this and that, covered in gloopy sauces. Henry checked under the tables to see if anyone was being sick yet.

There was no one lying poisoned under the tables. I guess it's just a matter of time, thought Henry grimly. You won't catch me eating anything here.

Mum, Dad, Peter and Rich Aunt Ruby blabbed away at their end of the table. Horrid Henry sat sullenly next to Stuck-Up Steve.

'I've got a new bike,' Steve bragged. 'Do you still have that old rust bucket you had last Christmas?'

'Hush, Steve,' said Rich Aunt Ruby.

Horrid Henry's foot got ready to kick Steve.

'Boudicca Battle-Axe! How many times have I told you – don't chew with your mouth open,' boomed a terrible voice.

Horrid Henry looked up. His jaw dropped.

There was his terrifying teacher, Miss Battle-Axe, sitting at a small table in the corner with her back to him. She was with someone even taller, skinnier, and more ferocious than she was.

'And take your elbows off the table!'

'Yes, Mum,' said Miss Battle-Axe meekly.

Henry could not believe his ears. Did teachers have mothers? Did teachers ever leave the school? Impossible.

'Boudicca! Stop slouching!'

'Yes, Mum,' said Miss Battle-Axe, straightening up a fraction.

'So, what's everyone having?' beamed Aunt Ruby. Horrid Henry tore his eyes away from Miss Battle-Axe and stared at the menu. It was entirely written in French.

'I recommend the mussels,' said Aunt Ruby.

'Mussels! Ick!' shrieked Henry.

'Or the blah blah blah blah blah.' Aunt Ruby pronounced a few mysterious French words.

'Maybe,' said Mum. She looked a little uncertain.

'Maybe,' said Dad. He looked a little uncertain.

'You order for me, Aunt Ruby,' said Perfect Peter. 'I eat everything.'

Horrid Henry had no idea what food Aunt Ruby had suggested, but he knew he hated every single thing on the menu.

'I want a burger,' said Henry.

'No burgers here,' said Mum firmly. 'This is Restaurant Le Posh.'

'I said I want a burger!' shouted Henry. Several diners looked up.

'Don't be horrid, Henry!' hissed Mum.

'I CAN'T UNDERSTAND THIS MENU!' screamed Henry.

'Calm down this minute Henry,' hissed Dad. 'Or no £2.'

Mum translated: 'A tasty . . . uh . . . something on a bed of roast something with a something sauce.'

'Sounds delicious,' said Dad.

'Wait, there's more,' said Mum. 'A big piece of something enrobed with something cooked in something with carrots.'

'Right, I'm having that,' said Dad. 'I love carrots.'

Mum carried on translating. Henry opened his mouth to scream –

'Why don't you order *tripe*?' said Steve.

'What's that?' asked Henry suspiciously.

'You don't want to know,' said Steve.

'Try me,' said Henry.

'Intestines,' said Steve. 'You know, the wriggly bits in your stomach.'

Horrid Henry snorted. Sometimes he felt sorry for Steve. Did Steve really think he'd fool him with *that* old trick? *Tripe* was probably a fancy French word for spaghetti. Or trifle.

'Or you could order *escargots*,' said Steve. 'I dare you.'

'What's *escargots*?' said Henry.

Stuck-Up Steve stuck his nose in the air.

'Oh, sorry, I forgot you don't learn French at your school. *I've* been learning it for years.'

'Whoopee for you,' said Horrid Henry.

'*Escargots* are snails, stupid,' said Stuck-Up Steve.

Steve must think he was a real idiot, thought Horrid Henry indignantly. *Snails.* Ha ha ha. In a restaurant? As if.

'Oh yeah, right, you big fat liar,' said Henry.

Steve shrugged.

'Too chicken, huh?' he sneered. 'Cluck cluck cluck.'

Horrid Henry was outraged. No one called him chicken and lived.

'Course not,' said Horrid Henry. 'I'd love to eat snails.' Naturally it would turn out to be fish or something in a smelly, disgusting sauce, but so what? *Escargots* could hardly be more revolting than all the other yucky things on the menu. Steve would have to try harder than that to fool him. He would order so-called 'snails' just to show Steve up for the liar he was. Then wouldn't he make fun of stupid old Steve!

'And vat are ve having tonight?' asked the French waiter.

Aunt Ruby ordered.

'An excellent choice, madame,' said the waiter.

Dad ordered. The waiter kissed his fingers.

'*Magnifique*, monsieur, our speciality.'

Mum ordered.

'Bravo, madame. And what about you, young man?' the waiter asked Henry.

'I'm having *escargots*,' said Henry.

'Hmmn,' said the waiter. 'Monsieur is a gourmet?'

Horrid Henry wasn't sure he liked the sound of that. Stuck-Up Steve snickered. What was going on? thought Horrid Henry.

'Boudicca! Eat your vegetables!'

'Yes, Mum.'

'Boudicca! Stop slurping.'

'Yes, Mum,' snapped Miss Battle-Axe.

'Boudicca! Don't pick your nose!'

'I wasn't!' said Miss Battle-Axe.

'Don't you contradict me,' said Mrs Battle-Axe.

The waiter reappeared, carrying six plates covered in silver domes.

'Voilà!' he said, whisking off the lids with a flourish. '*Bon appétit!*'

Everyone peered at their elegant plates.

'Ah,' said Mum, looking at her squid.

'Ah,' said Dad, looking at his stuffed tomatoes.

'Ah,' said Peter, looking at his beetroot mousse.

Horrid Henry stared at his food. It looked like —

it couldn't be — oh my God, it was . . . SNAILS! It
really was snails! Squishy squashy squidgy slimy
slithery slippery snails. Still in their shells. Drenched
in butter, but unmistakably snails. Steve had tricked
him.

Horrid Henry's hand reached out to hurl the snails
at Steve.

Stuck-Up Steve giggled.

Horrid Henry stopped and gritted his teeth. No
way was he giving Steve the satisfaction of seeing him
get into big trouble. He'd ordered snails and he'd eat
snails. And when he threw up, he'd make sure it was
all over Steve.

Horrid Henry grabbed his fork and plunged. Then
he closed his eyes and popped the snail in his mouth.

Horrid Henry chewed.

Horrid Henry chewed some more.

'Hmmn,' said Horrid Henry.

He popped another snail in his mouth. And another.

'Yummy,' said Henry. 'This is brilliant.' Why hadn't anyone told him that Le Posh served such thrillingly revolting food? Wait till he told Rude Ralph!

Stuck-Up Steve looked unhappy.

'How's your maggot sauce, Steve?' said Henry cheerfully.

'It's not maggot sauce,' said Steve.

'Maggot maggot maggot,' whispered Henry. 'Watch them wriggle about.'

Steve put down his fork. So did Mum, Dad, and Peter.

'Go on everyone, eat up,' said Henry, chomping.

'I'm not that hungry,' said Mum.

'You said we had to eat everything on our plate,' said Henry.

'No I didn't,' said Dad weakly.

'You did too!' said Henry. 'So eat!'

'I don't like beetroot,' moaned Perfect Peter.

'Hush, Peter,' snapped Mum.

'Peter, I never thought *you* were a fussy eater,' said Aunt Ruby.

'I'm not!' wailed Perfect Peter.

'Boudicca!' blasted Mrs Battle-Axe's shrill voice. 'Pay attention when I'm speaking to you!'

'Yes, Mum,' said Miss Battle-Axe.

'Why can't you be as good as that boy?' said Mrs Battle-Axe, pointing to Horrid Henry. 'Look at him sitting there, eating so beautifully.'

Miss Battle-Axe turned round and saw Henry. Her face went bright red, then purple, then white. She gave him a sickly smile.

Horrid Henry gave her a little polite wave. Oh boy.

For the first time in his life was he ever looking forward to school.

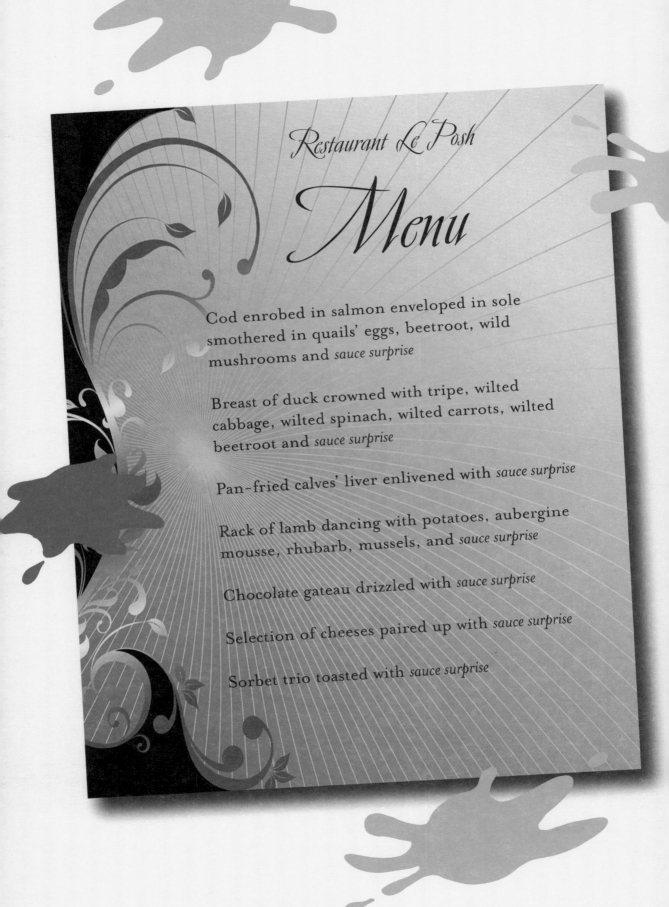

Restaurant Le Posh

Menu

Cod enrobed in salmon enveloped in sole smothered in quails' eggs, beetroot, wild mushrooms and *sauce surprise*

Breast of duck crowned with tripe, wilted cabbage, wilted spinach, wilted carrots, wilted beetroot and *sauce surprise*

Pan-fried calves' liver enlivened with *sauce surprise*

Rack of lamb dancing with potatoes, aubergine mousse, rhubarb, mussels, and *sauce surprise*

Chocolate gateau drizzled with *sauce surprise*

Selection of cheeses paired up with *sauce surprise*

Sorbet trio toasted with *sauce surprise*

HORRiD HENRY'S
Ambush

It was Christmas Eve at last. Every minute felt like an hour. Every hour felt like a year. How could Henry live until Christmas morning when he could get his hands on all his loot?

Mum and Dad were baking frantically in the kitchen.

Perfect Peter sat by the twinkling Christmas tree scratching out 'Silent Night' over and over again on his cello.

'Can't you play something else?' snapped Henry.

'No,' said Peter, sawing away. 'This is the only Christmas carol I know. You can move if you don't like it.'

'You move,' said Henry.

Peter ignored him.

'Siiiiiiiii—lent Niiiiight,' screeched the cello.

AAARRRGH.

Horrid Henry lay on the sofa with his fingers in his ears, double-checking his choices from the Toy Heaven catalogue. Big red 'X's' appeared on every page, to help you-know-who remember all the toys he absolutely had to have. Oh please, let everything he wanted leap from its pages and into Santa's sack. After all, what could be better than looking at a huge glittering stack of presents on Christmas morning, and knowing that they were all for you?

Oh please let this be the year when he finally got everything he wanted!

His letter to Father Christmas couldn't have been clearer.

323

Dear Father Christmas

I want loads and loads of cash, to make up for the puny ammount you put in my stocking last year. And a Robomatic Supersonic Space Howler Deluxe plus attachments would be great, too. I have asked for this before, you know! And the Terminator Gladiator fighting kit. I need lots more Day-Glo Slime and comics and a Mutant Max poster and the new Zapatron HipHop Dinosaur. This is your <u>last chance</u>.

Henry

P.S. Satzumas are NOT presents!!!

P.P.S Peter asked me to tell you to give me all his presents as he doesn't want any.

How hard could it be for Father Christmas to get this right? He'd asked for the Space Howler last year, and it never arrived. Instead, Henry got . . . vests. And handkerchiefs. And books. And

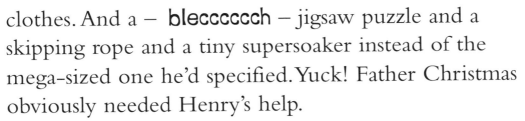

clothes. And a – **bleccccch** – jigsaw puzzle and a skipping rope and a tiny supersoaker instead of the mega-sized one he'd specified. Yuck! Father Christmas obviously needed Henry's help.

Father Christmas is getting old and doddery, thought Henry. Maybe he hasn't got my letters. Maybe he's lost his reading glasses. Or – what a horrible thought – maybe he was delivering Henry's presents by mistake to some other Henry. Eeeek! Some yucky, undeserving Henry was probably right now this minute playing with Henry's Terminator Gladiator sword, shield, axe, and trident. And enjoying his Intergalactic Samurai Gorillas. It was so unfair!

And then suddenly Henry had a brilliant, spectacular idea. Why had he never thought of this before? All his present problems would be over.

Presents were far too important to leave to Father Christmas. Since he couldn't be trusted to bring the right gifts, Horrid Henry had no choice. He would have to ambush Father Christmas.

Yes!

He'd hold Father Christmas hostage with his Goo-Shooter, while he rummaged in his present sack for all the loot he was owed. Maybe Henry would keep the lot. Now *that* would be fair.

Let's see, thought Horrid Henry. Father Christmas was bound to be a slippery character, so he'd need to booby-trap his bedroom. When you-know-who sneaked in to fill his stocking at the end of the bed, Henry could leap up and nab him. Father Christmas had a lot of explaining to do for all those years of stockings filled with satsumas and walnuts instead of chocolate and cold hard cash.

So, how best to capture him?

Henry considered.

A bucket of water above the door.

A skipping rope stretched tight across the entrance, guaranteed to trip up intruders.

A web of string criss-crossed from bedpost to door and threaded with bells to ensnare night-time visitors.

And let's not forget strategically scattered whoopee cushions.

His plan was foolproof.

Loot, here I come, thought Horrid Henry.

Horrid Henry sat up in bed, his Goo-Shooter aimed at the half-open door where a bucket of water balanced. All his traps were laid. No one was getting in without Henry knowing about it. Any minute now, he'd catch Father Christmas and make him pay up.

Henry waited. And waited. And waited. His eyes started to feel heavy and he closed them for a moment.

There was a rustling at Henry's door.

Oh my god, this was it! Henry lay down and pretended to be asleep.

Cr-eeeek.

Cr-eeeek.

Horrid Henry reached for his Goo-Shooter.

A huge shape loomed in the doorway.

Henry braced himself to attack.

'Doesn't he look sweet when he's asleep?' whispered the shape.

'What a little snugglechops,' whispered another.

Sweet? Snugglechops?

Horrid Henry's fingers itched to let Mum and Dad have it with both barrels. **Pow! Splat!**

Henry could see it now. Mum covered in green goo. Dad covered in green goo. Mum and Dad snatching the Goo-Shooter and wrecking all his plans and throwing out all his presents and banning him from TV for ever . . . hmmmn. His fingers felt a little less itchy.

Henry lowered his Goo-Shooter. The bucket of water wobbled above the door.

Yikes! What if Mum and Dad stepped into his Santa traps? All his hard work – ruined.

'I'm awake,' snarled Henry.

The shapes stepped back. The water stopped wobbling.

'Go to sleep!' hissed Mum.

'Go to sleep!' hissed Dad.

'What are you doing here?' demanded Henry.

'Checking on you,' said Mum. 'Now go to sleep or Father Christmas will never come.'

He'd better, thought Henry.

Horrid Henry woke with a jolt.

AAARRGGH! He'd fallen asleep. How could he? Panting and gasping Henry switched on the light. Phew. His traps were intact. His stocking was empty. Father Christmas hadn't been yet.

Wow, was that lucky. That was incredibly lucky. Henry lay back, his heart pounding. And then Horrid Henry had a terrible thought.

What if Father Christmas had decided to be spiteful and *avoid* Henry's bedroom this year? Or what if he'd played a sneaky trick on Henry and filled a stocking *downstairs* instead?

Nah. No way.

But wait. When Father Christmas came to Rude Ralph's house he always filled the stockings downstairs. Now Henry came to think of it, Moody

Margaret always left her stocking downstairs too, hanging from the fireplace, not from the end of her bed, like Henry did.

Horrid Henry looked at the clock. It was past midnight. Mum and Dad had forbidden him to go downstairs till morning, on pain of having all his presents taken away and no telly all day.

But this was an emergency. He'd creep downstairs, take a quick peek to make sure he hadn't missed Father Christmas, then be back in bed in a jiffy.

No one will ever know, thought Horrid Henry.

Henry tiptoed round the whoopee cushions, leaped over the criss-cross threads, stepped over the skipping rope and carefully squeezed through his door so as not to disturb the bucket of water. Then he crept downstairs.

Sneak

Sneak

Sneak

Horrid Henry shone his torch over the sitting room. Father Christmas hadn't been. The room was exactly as he'd left it that evening.

Except for one thing. Henry's light illuminated the Christmas tree, heavy with chocolate santas and chocolate bells and chocolate reindeer. Mum and Dad must have hung them on the tree after he'd gone to bed.

Horrid Henry looked at the chocolates cluttering up the Christmas tree. Shame, thought Horrid Henry, the way those chocolates spoil the view of all those lovely decorations. You could barely see the baubles and tinsel he and Peter had worked so hard to put on.

'Hi, Henry,' said the chocolate santas. 'Don't you want to eat us?'

'Go on, Henry,' said the chocolate bells. 'You know you want to.'

'What are you waiting for, Henry?' urged the chocolate reindeer.

What indeed? After all, it *was* Christmas.

Henry took a chocolate santa or three from the side, and then another two from the back. Hmmn, boy, was that great chocolate, he thought, stuffing them into his mouth.

Oops. Now the chocolate santas looked a little unbalanced.

Better take a few from the front and from the other side, to even it up, thought Henry. Then no one will notice there are a few chocolates missing.

Henry gobbled and gorged and guzzled. Wow, were those chocolates yummy!!!

The tree looks a bit bare, thought Henry a little while later. Mum had such eagle eyes she might notice that a few – well, all – of the chocolates were missing. He'd better hide all those gaps with a few extra baubles. And, while he was improving the tree, he could swap that stupid fairy for Terminator Gladiator.

Henry piled extra decorations onto the branches. Soon the Christmas tree was so covered in baubles and tinsel there was barely a hint of green. No one would notice the missing chocolates. Then Henry stood on a chair, dumped the fairy, and, standing on his tippy-tippy toes, hung Terminator Gladiator at the top where he belonged.

Perfect, thought Horrid Henry, jumping off the chair and stepping back to admire his work. Absolutely perfect. Thanks to me this is the best tree ever.

There was a terrible creaking sound. Then another. Then suddenly . . .

CRASH!

The Christmas tree toppled over.

Horrid Henry's heart stopped.

Upstairs he could hear Mum and Dad stirring.

'Oy! Who's down there?' shouted Dad.

RUN!!! thought Horrid Henry. Run for your life!!

Horrid Henry ran like he had never run before, up the stairs to his room before Mum and Dad could catch him. Oh please let him get there in time. His parents' bedroom door opened just as Henry dashed inside his room. He'd made it. He was safe.

Splash! The bucket of water spilled all over him.

Trip! Horrid Henry fell over the skipping rope.

Crash! Smash! Ring! Ring! jangled the bells.

PLLLLLLL! belched the whoopee cushions.

'What is going on in here?' shrieked Mum, glaring.

'Nothing,' said Horrid Henry, as he lay sprawled on the floor soaking wet and tangled up in threads

and wires and rope. 'I heard a noise downstairs so I got up to check,' he added innocently.

'Tree's fallen over,' called Dad. 'Must have been overloaded. Don't worry, I'll sort it.'

'Get back to bed, Henry,' said Mum wearily. 'And don't touch your stocking till morning.'

Henry looked. And gasped. His stocking was stuffed and bulging. That mean old sneak, thought Horrid Henry indignantly. How did he do it? How had he escaped the traps?

Watch out Father Christmas, thought Horrid Henry. I'll get you next year.

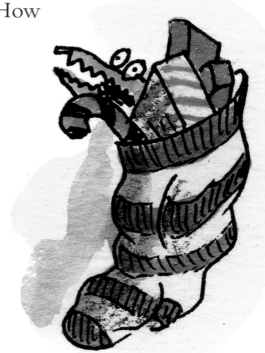

Santa traps

DON'T LET SANTA GET AWAY –
HOLD HIM HOSTAGE TO MAKE
SURE YOU GET THE GIFTS
YOU DESERVE.

1. Hold him hostage with your Goo-Shooter or Super-Soaker so you can go through his present sack to find all those presents he keeps forgetting to give you.

2. Booby-trap the area in front of the fireplace where the stockings are hung and nab him.

3. Scatter whoopee cushions by the chimney so he can't sneak past you.

4. Whatever you do, don't block the chimney! Let Santa in first, then nab him.

Pssst: Peters real name is
Poopsicle Worm the Third
I'm telling on you!
Go ahead,
Poopsicle Wormy Worm

HORRID HENRY'S
Rainy Day

Horrid Henry was bored. Horrid Henry was fed up. He'd been banned from the computer for rampaging through Our Town Museum. He'd been banned from watching TV just because he was caught watching a *teeny* tiny bit extra after he'd been told to switch it off straight after Mutant Max. Could he help it if an exciting new series about a rebel robot had started right after? How would he know if it were any good unless he watched some of it?

It was completely unfair and all Peter's fault for telling on him, and Mum and Dad were the meanest, most horrible parents in the world.

And now he was stuck indoors, all day long, with absolutely nothing to do.

The rain splattered down. The house was grey. The world was grey. The universe was grey.

'I'm bored!' wailed Horrid Henry.

'Read a book,' said Mum.

'Do your homework,' said Dad.

'NO!' said Horrid Henry.

'Then tidy your room,' said Mum.

'Unload the dishwasher,' said Dad.

'Empty the bins,' said Mum.

'NO WAY!' shrieked Horrid Henry. What was he, a slave? Better keep out of his parents' way, or they'd come up with even more horrible things for him to do.

Horrid Henry stomped up to his boring bedroom and slammed the door. Uggh. He hated all his toys. He hated all his music. He hated all his games.

UGGGHHHHHH! What could he do?

Aha.

He could always check to see what Peter was up to.

Perfect Peter was sitting in his room arranging stamps in his stamp album.

'Peter is a baby, Peter is a baby,' jeered Horrid Henry, sticking his head round the door.

'Don't call me baby,' said Perfect Peter.

'OK, Duke of Poop,' said Henry.

'Don't call me Duke!' shrieked Peter.

'OK, Poopsicle,' said Henry.

'MUUUUM!' wailed Peter. 'Henry called me Poopsicle!'

'Don't be horrid, Henry!' shouted Mum. 'Stop calling your brother names.'

Horrid Henry smiled sweetly at Peter.

'OK, Peter, 'cause I'm so nice, I'll let you make a list of ten names that you don't want to be called,' said Henry. 'And it will only cost you £1.'

£1! Perfect Peter could not believe his ears. Peter would pay much more than that never to be called Poopsicle again.

'Is this a trick, Henry?' said Peter.

'No,' said Henry. 'How dare you? I make you a good offer, and you accuse me. Well, just for that—'

'Wait,' said Peter. 'I accept.' He handed Henry a pound coin. At last, all those horrid names would be banned. Henry would never call him Duke of Poop again.

Peter got out a piece of paper and a pencil.

Now, let's see, what to put on the list, thought Peter. Poopsicle, for a start. And I hate being called Baby, and Nappy Face, and Duke of Poop.
Peter wrote and wrote and wrote.

'OK, Henry, here's the list,' said Peter.

NAMES I DON'T WANT TO BE CALLED

1. Poopsicle
2. Duke of Poop
3. Ugly
4. Nappy face
5. Baby
6 Toad
7. Smelly toad
8. Ugg
9. Worm
10. Wibble pants

Horrid Henry scanned the list. 'Fine, pongy pants,' said Henry. 'Sorry, I meant poopy pants. Or was it smelly nappy?'

'MUUUMM!' wailed Peter. 'Henry's calling me names!'

'Henry!' screamed Mum. 'For the last time, can't you leave your brother alone?'

Horrid Henry considered. *Could* he leave that worm alone?

'Peter is a frog, Peter is a frog,' chanted Henry.

'MUUUUUUMMMMM!' screamed Peter.

'That's it, Henry!' shouted Mum. 'No pocket money for a week. Go to your room and stay there.'

'Fine!' shrieked Henry. 'You'll all be sorry when I'm dead.' He stomped down the hall and slammed his bedroom door as hard as he could. *Why* were his parents so mean and horrible? He was hardly bothering Peter at all. Peter *was* a frog. Henry was only telling the truth.

Boy would they be sorry when he'd died of boredom stuck up here.

If only we'd let him watch a little extra TV, Mum would wail. Would that have been so terrible?

If only we hadn't made him do any chores, Dad would sob.

Why didn't I let Henry call me names, Peter would howl. After all, I do have smelly pants.

And now it's too late and we're sooooooo sorry, they would shriek.

But wait. *Would* they be sorry? Peter would grab his room. And all his best toys. His arch-enemy Stuck-Up Steve could come over and snatch anything he wanted, even his skeleton bank and Goo-Shooter. Peter could invade the Purple Hand fort and Henry couldn't stop him. Moody Margaret could hop over the wall and nick his flag. And his biscuits. And his Dungeon Drink Kit. Even his . . . Supersoaker.

NOOOOOO!!!
Horrid Henry went pale. He had to stop those rapacious thieves.

But how?

I could come back and haunt them, thought Horrid Henry. Yes! That would teach those grave-robbers not to mess with me.

'OOOOOOO, get out of my rooooooooooom, you horrrrrrrible tooooooooooooad,' he would moan at Peter.

'Touch my Goooooooo-Shoooooter and you'll be morphed into ectoplasm,' he'd groan spookily from under Stuck-Up Steve's bed. Ha! That would show him.

Or he'd pop out from inside Moody Margaret's wardrobe.

'Giiiiive Henrrrrry's toyyyys back, you mis-er-a-ble sliiiiiimy snake,' he would rasp. That would teach her a thing or two.

Henry smiled. But fun as it would be to haunt people, he'd rather stop horrible enemies snatching his stuff in the first place.

And then suddenly Horrid Henry had a brilliant, spectacular idea. Hadn't Mum told him just the other day that people wrote wills to say who they wanted to get all their stuff when they died? Henry had been thrilled.

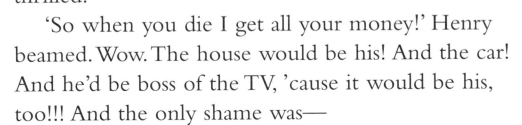

'So when you die I get all your money!' Henry beamed. Wow. The house would be his! And the car! And he'd be boss of the TV, 'cause it would be his, too!!! And the only shame was—

'Couldn't you just give it all to me now?' asked Henry.

'Henry!' snapped Mum. 'Don't be horrid.'

There was no time to lose. He had to write a will immediately.

Horrid Henry sat down at his desk and grabbed some paper.

MY WILL

**WARNING: DO NOT READ UNLESS
I AM DEAD!!!! I mean it!!!!**

If you're reading this it's because I'm dead and you aren't. I wish you were dead and I wasn't, so I could have all your stuff. It's so not fair.

First of all, to anyone thinking of snatching my stuff just 'cause I'm dead ... BEWARE! Anyone who doesn't do what I say will get haunted by a bloodless and boneless ghoul, namely me. So there.

Now the hard bit, thought Horrid Henry. Who should get his things? Was anyone deserving enough?

Peter, you are a worm. And a toad. And an ugly baby nappy face smelly ugg wibble pants poopsicle. I leave you ...hmmmn. That toad really shouldn't get anything. But Peter was his brother after all. I leave you my sweet wrappers. And a muddy twig.

That was more than Peter deserved. Still . . .

Steve, you are stuck-up and horrible and the world's worst cousin. You can have a pair of my socks. You can choose the blue ones with the holes or the falling down orange ones.

Margaret, you nit-face. I give you the Purple Hand flag to remember me by—NOT! You can have two radishes and the knight with the

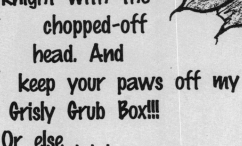

chopped-off head. And keep your paws off my Grisly Grub Box!!! Or else . . .

Miss Battle-Axe, you are my worst teacher ever. I leave you a broken pencil.

Aunt Ruby, you can have the lime green cardigan back that you gave me for Christmas.

Hmmm. So far he wasn't doing so well giving away any of his good things.

> Ralph, you can have my Goo-Shooter, but ONLY if you give me your football and your bike and your computer game Slime Ghouls.

That was more like it. After all, why should he be the only one writing a will? It was certainly a lot more fun thinking about *getting* stuff from other people than giving away his own treasures.

In fact, wouldn't he be better off helping others by telling them what he wanted? Wouldn't it be awful if Rich Aunt Ruby left him some of Steve's old clothes in her will thinking that he would be delighted? Better write to her at once.

Now, Steve. Henry was leaving him an old pair of holey socks. But Steve didn't have to *know* that, did he. For all Henry knew, Steve *loved* holey socks.

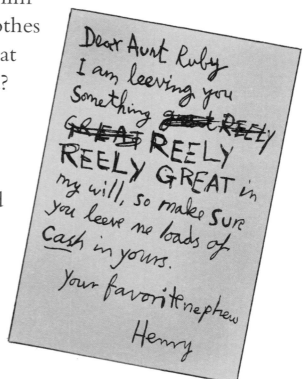

Dear Aunt Ruby
I am leeving you Something ~~grat~~ ~~reely~~ ~~GREAT~~ REELY REELY GREAT in my will, so make sure you leeve me loads of cash in yours.
Your favorite nephew
Henry

Dear Steve

You know your new blue racing bike with the silver trim? Well when your dead it wont be any use to you, So please leave it to me in your will
Your favourite cousin
Henry

P.S. By the way, no need to wait till your dead, You can give it to me now.

Right, Mum and Dad.
When they were in the
old people's home they'd
hardly need a thing.
A rocking chair and
blanket each would
do fine for them.
So, how would
Dad's music system
look in his bedroom?
And where could he
put Mum's clock radio?
Henry had always liked the chiming clock
on their mantelpiece and the picture of the blackbird.
Better go and check to see where he could put them.

Henry went into Mum and Dad's room, and grabbed an armload of stuff. He staggered to his bedroom and dumped everything on the floor, then went back for a second helping.

Stumbling and staggering under his heavy burden, Horrid Henry swayed down the hall and crashed into Dad.

'What are you doing?' said Dad, staring. 'That's mine.'

'And those are mine,' said Mum.

'What is going on?' shrieked Mum and Dad.

'I was just checking how all this stuff will look in my room when you're in the old people's home,' said Horrid Henry.

'I'm not there yet,' said Mum.

'Put everything back,' said Dad.

Horrid Henry scowled. Here he was, just trying to think ahead, and he gets told off.

'Well, just for that I won't leave you any of my knights in my will,' said Henry.

Honestly, some people were so selfish.

Dear Mum and Dad
Make sure you leave me all your money in your will (Peter says he doesn't want any).

Love from your favourite son

Henry

P.S. Don't forget to make your will as soon as possible

Dear Great-Aunt Greta
Since you are really really old and don't need anything. Why not give all your money to me?

Love from your very very poor nephew

Henry

Margaret
You have been mean and horrid to me for years. Why not say you're sorry by leaving me all your pirate hats and eye patches and cutlasses and snickersnees in your will? In fact, no need to wait until you're dead – you can say sorry by giving them all to me RIGHT NOW!

Henry

PERFECT PETER'S
Pirate Party

'N ow, let's see,' said Mum, consulting her list, 'we need pirate flags, pieces of eight, swords, treasure chests, eyepatches, skull and crossbones plates. Have I missed anything?'

Horrid Henry stopped chewing. Wow! For once, Mum was talking about something important. His Purple Hand Pirate party wasn't till next month, but it was never too soon to start getting in supplies for the birthday party of the year. No, the century.

But wait. Mum had forgotten cutlasses. They were essential for the gigantic pirate battle Henry was planning. And what about all the ketchup for fake blood? And where were the buckets of sweets?

Horrid Henry opened his mouth to speak.

'That sounds great, Mum,' piped Perfect Peter. 'But don't forget the pirate napkins.'

'Napkins. Check,' said Mum, smiling.

Huh?

'I don't want napkins at my party,' said Horrid Henry.

'This isn't for your party,' said Mum. 'It's for Peter's.'

356

WHAT???

'What do you mean, it's for Peter's?' gasped Horrid Henry. He felt as if an icy hand had gripped him by the throat. He was having trouble breathing.

'Peter's birthday is next week, and he's having a pirate party,' said Mum.

Perfect Peter kept eating his muesli.

'But he's having a Sammy the Snail party,' said Horrid Henry, glaring at Peter.

'I changed my mind,' said Perfect Peter.

'But pirates was *my* party idea!' shrieked Horrid Henry. 'I've been planning it for months. You're just a copycat.'

'You don't own pirates,' said Peter. 'Gordon had a pirate party for *his* birthday. So I want pirates for mine.'

'Henry, you can still have a pirate party,' said Dad.

'NOOOOOO!' screamed Horrid Henry. He couldn't have a pirate party *after* Peter. Everyone would think he'd copied his wormy toad brother.

Henry pounced. He was a poisoned arrow whizzing towards its target.

THUD! Peter fell off his chair.

SMASH! Peter's muesli bowl crashed to the floor.

'**AAAEEEIIIII!**' screeched Perfect Peter.

'Look what you've done, you horrid boy!' yelled Mum. 'Say sorry to Peter.'

'**WAAAAAAAAAAA!**' sobbed Peter.

'I won't!' said Horrid Henry. 'I'm not sorry. He stole my party idea, and I hate him.'

'Then go to your room and stay there,' said Dad.

'It's not fair!' wailed Horrid Henry.

'What shall we do with the drunken sailor? What shall we do with the drunken sailor?' sang Perfect Peter as he walked past Henry's slammed bedroom door.

'Make him walk the plank!' screamed Horrid Henry. 'Which is what will happen to you if you don't SHUT UP!'

'Muum! Henry told me to shut up,' yelled Peter.

'Henry! Leave your brother alone,' said Mum.

'You're the eldest. Can't you be grown-up for once and let him have his party in peace?' said Dad.

NO! thought Horrid Henry. He could not. He had to stop Peter having a pirate party. He just had to.

But how?

He could bribe Peter. But that would cost money that Henry didn't have. He could promise to be nice to him . . . No way. That was going too far. That little copycat worm did not deserve Henry's niceness.

Maybe he could *trick* him into abandoning his party idea. Hmmmm. Henry smiled. Hmmmmm.

Horrid Henry opened Peter's bedroom door and sauntered in. Perfect Peter was busy writing names on his YO HO HO pirate invitations. The same ones, Henry noticed, that *he'd* been planning to send, with the peg-legged pirate swirling his cutlass and looking like he was about to leap out at you.

'You're supposed to be in your room,' said Peter. 'I'm telling on you.'

'You know, Peter, I'm glad you're having a pirate party,' said Henry.

Peter paused.

'You are?' said Peter cautiously.

'Yeah,' said Horrid Henry. 'It means you'll get the pirate cannibal curse and I won't.'

'There's no such thing as a pirate cannibal curse,' said Peter.

'Fine,' said Horrid Henry. 'Just don't blame me when you end up as a shrunken head dangling round a cannibal's neck.'

Henry's such a liar, thought Peter. He's just trying to scare me.

'Gordon had a pirate party, and *he* didn't turn into a shrunken head,' said Peter.

Henry sighed.

'Of course not, because his name doesn't start with P. The cannibal pirate who made the curse was named Blood Boil Bob. Look, that's him on the invitations,' said Henry.

Peter glanced at the pirate. Was it his imagination, or did Blood Boil Bob have an especially mean and hungry look? Peter put down his crayon.

'He had a hateful younger brother named Paul, who became Blood Boil Bob's first shrunken head,' said Henry. 'Since then, the cannibal curse has passed down to anyone else whose name starts with P.'

'I don't believe you, Henry,' said Peter. He was sure Henry was trying to trick him. Lots of his friends had had pirate parties, and none of them had turned into a shrunken head.

On the other hand, none of his friends had names that began with P.

'How does the curse happen?' said Peter slowly.

Horrid Henry looked around. Then, putting a finger to his lips, he crept over to Peter's wardrobe and flung it open. Peter jumped.

'Just checking Blood Boil Bob's not in there,' whispered Henry. 'Now keep your voice down. Remember, dressing up as pirates, singing pirate songs, talking about treasure, wakes up the pirate cannibal. Sometimes – if you're lucky – he just steals all the treasure. Other times he . . . POUNCES,' shrieked Henry.

Peter turned pale.

'Yo ho, yo ho, a pirate's life for me,' sang Horrid Henry. 'Yo ho — whoops, sorry, better not sing, in case *he* turns up.'

'MUUUMMM!' wailed Peter. 'Henry's trying to scare me!'

'What's going on?' said Mum.

'Henry said I'm going to turn into a shrunken head if I have a pirate party.'

'Henry, don't be horrid,' said Mum, glaring. 'Peter, there's no such thing.'

'Told you, Henry,' said Perfect Peter.

'If I were you I'd have a Sammy the Slug party,' said Horrid Henry.

'Sammy the *Snail*,' said Peter. 'I'm having a pirate party and you can't stop me. So there.'

Rats, thought Horrid Henry. How could he make Peter change his mind?

'Don't **dooooooo** **it**, Peter,' Henry howled spookily under Peter's door every night. 'Beware! Beware!'

'Stop it, Henry!' screamed Peter.

'You'll be sorry,' Horrid Henry scrawled all over Peter's homework.

'Remember the cannibal curse,' Henry whispered over supper the night before the party.

'Henry, leave your brother alone or you won't be coming to the party,' said Mum.

What? Miss out on chocolate pieces of eight? Henry scowled. That was the least he was owed.

It was so unfair. Why did Peter have to wreck everything?

It was Peter's birthday party. Mum and Dad hung two huge skull and crossbones pirate flags outside the house. The exact ones, Horrid Henry noted bitterly, that he had planned for *his* birthday party. The cutlasses had been decorated and the galleon cake eaten. All that remained was for Peter's horrible guests, Tidy Ted, Spotless Sam, Goody-Goody Gordon, Perky Parveen, Helpful Hari, Tell-Tale Tim and Mini Minnie to go on the treasure hunt.

'Yo ho, yo ho, a pirate's life for me,' sang Horrid Henry. He was wearing his pirate skull scarf, his eyepatch, and his huge black skull and crossbones hat. His bloody cutlass gleamed.

'Don't sing that,' said Peter.

'Why not, baby?' said Henry.

'You know why,' muttered Peter.

'I warned you about Blood Boil Bob, but you wouldn't listen,' hissed Henry, 'and now—' he drew his hand across his throat. 'Hey everyone, let's play pin the tail on Peter.'

'MUUUUUUUUMMMMMM!' wailed Peter.

'Behave yourself, Henry,' muttered Mum, 'or you won't be coming on the treasure hunt.'

Henry scowled. The only reason he was even at this baby party was because the treasure chest was filled with chocolate pieces of eight.

Mum clapped her hands.

'Come on everyone, look for the clues hidden around the house to help you find the pirate treasure,' she said, handing Peter a scroll. 'Here's the first one.'

Climb the stair,
if you dare,
you'll find a clue,
just for you.

'I found a clue,' squealed Helpful Hari, grabbing the scroll dangling from the banister.

Turn to the left,
turn to the right,
reach into the bag,
don't get a fright.

The party pounded off to the left, then to the right, where another scroll hung in a pouch from Peter's doorknob.

'I found the treasure map!' shouted Perky Parveen.

'Oh goody,' said Goody-Goody Gordon.

Everyone gathered round the ancient scroll.

'It says to go to the park,' squealed Spotless Sam. 'Look, X marks the spot where the treasure is buried.'

Dad, waving a skull and crossbones flag, led the pirates out of the door and down the road to the park.

Horrid Henry ran ahead through the park gates and took off his skull and crossbones hat and eyepatch. No way did he want anyone to think he was part of this *baby* pirate party. He glanced at the swings. Was there anyone here that he knew? Phew, no one, just some little girl on the slide.

The little girl looked up and stared at Horrid Henry. Horrid Henry stared back.

Uh oh.

Oh no.

Henry began to back away. But it was too late.

'Henwy!' squealed the little girl. 'Henwy!'

It was Lisping Lily, New Nick's horrible sister. Henry had met her on the world's worst sleepover at Nick's house, where she—where she—

'Henwy! I love you, Henwy!' squealed Lisping Lily, running towards him. 'Will you marry with me, Henwy?'

Horrid Henry turned and ran down the windy path into the gardens. Lisping Lily ran after him. 'Henwy! Henwy!'

Henry dived into some thick bushes and crouched behind them.

Please don't find me, please don't find me, he prayed.

Henry waited, his heart pounding. All he could hear was Peter's pirate party, advancing his way. Had he lost her?

'I think the treasure's over there!' shouted Peter.

Phew. He'd ditched her. He was safe.

'Henwy?' came a little voice. 'Henwy! Where are you? I want to give you a big kiss.'

AAAARRGGHH!

Then Horrid Henry remembered who he was. The boy who'd got Miss Battle-Axe sent to the head. The boy who'd defeated the demon dinner lady. The boy who was scared of nothing (except injections). What was a pirate king like him doing hiding from some tiddly toddler?

Horrid Henry put on his pirate hat and grabbed his cutlass. He'd scare her off if it was the last thing he did.

'AAAAARRRRRRRRRRR!' roared the pirate king, leaping up and brandishing his bloody cutlass.

'AAAAAAAAHHH!' squealed Lisping Lily. She turned and ran, crashing into Peter.

'Piwates! Piwates!' she screamed, dashing away.

Perfect Peter's blood ran cold. He looked into the thrashing bushes and saw a skull and crossbones rising out of the hedge, the gleam of sunlight on a blood-red cutlass...

'AAAAAAAAHHHHHH!' screamed Peter. 'It's Blood Boil Bob!' He turned and ran.

'AAAAAAAAHHHHHH!' shrieked Ted. He turned and ran.

'AAAAAAAAHHHHHH!' shrieked Gordon, Parveen, and the rest. They turned and ran.

Huh? thought Horrid Henry, trying to wriggle free.

Thud!

Henry's foot knocked against something hard. There, hidden beneath some leaves under the hedge, was a pirate chest.

Eureka!

'Help!' shrieked Perfect Peter. 'Help! Help!'

Mum and Dad ran over.

'What's happened?'

'We got attacked by pirates!' wailed Parveen.

'We ran for our lives!' wailed Gordon.

'Pirates?' said Mum.

'Pirates?' said Dad. 'How many were there?'

'Five!'

'Ten!'

'Hundreds!' wailed Mini Minnie.

'Don't be silly,' said Mum.

'I'm sure they're gone now, so let's find the treasure,' said Dad.

Peter opened the map and headed for the hedge nearest to the gate where the treasure map showed a giant X.

'I'm too scared,' he whimpered.

Helpful Hari crept to the treasure chest and lifted the lid. Everyone gasped. All that was left inside were a few crumpled gold wrappers.

'The treasure's gone,' whispered Peter.

Just then Horrid Henry sauntered along the path, twirling his hat.

'Where have you been?' said Mum.

'Hiding,' said Horrid Henry truthfully.

'We got raided,' gasped Ted.

'By pirates,' gasped Gordon.

'No way,' said Horrid Henry.

'They stole all the pieces of eight,' wailed Peter.

Horrid Henry sighed.

'What did I tell you about the cannibal curse?' he said. 'Just be glad you've still got your heads.'

Hmmmm, boy, chocolate pieces of eight were always yummy, but raided pieces of eight tasted even better, thought Horrid Henry that night, shoving a few more chocolates into his mouth.

Come to think of it, there'd been too many pirate parties recently.

Now, a cannibal curse party . . . Hmmmn.

Come to Henry's
Cannibal Curse
Birthday Party

PARTY MENU
Chocolate Eyeballs

Jelly bellies

Liquorice hair

PARTY GAMES
Bobbing for eyeballs

Bash the brain

Bogey-eating contest

Whack the skull off the skeleton

Shrink Peter's head

HORRID HENRY'S
Top Secret Fact File

Best Parties
Pirate parties
Cannibal curse parties
Terminator Gladiator parties

Worst Parties
Sammy the Snail party
Daffy and her Dancing
Daisies party
Princess party

Best Wedding
NONE!

Worst Wedding
Marrying Miss
Battle-Axe

Best Dinner Guests
Terminator Gladiator
Mutant Max
Marvin the Maniac
Tapioca Tina
Rapper Zapper

Worst Dinner Guests

Miss Battle-Axe
Stuck-Up Steve
Demon Dinner Lady

Best Revenge

Telling Peter there were fairies
at the bottom of the garden
Making Peter believe he was
famous in the future
Getting Bossy Bill into trouble
Making Steve think there were
monsters under the bed

Worst Revenge

Peter sending Margaret a letter signed 'Henry' asking
her to marry him (uggh)

Best Hike

Walking between the
comfy black chair
and the fridge

Worst Hike

Anywhere outdoors

Best Sleepovers
Eating all the ice cream at Greedy Graham's
Breaking all the beds at Dizzy Dave's
Staying up all night at Rude Ralph's

Worst Sleepovers
New Nick
Stuck-Up Steve
Moody Margaret nabbing my room

Best Will
Anyone leaving me lots of loot

Worst Will
Mine

Best Restaurants
Gobble and Go
Whopper Whoopee
Fat Frank's

Worst Restaurants
Restaurant Le Posh
Virtuous Veggie

the Virtuous Veggie
The all new Vegetable restaurant